There's A Branch
Near You

HARRIS COUNTY PUBLIC LIBRARY

HOUSTON, TEXAS

Cry, Coyote

Cry, Coyote

STEVE FRAZEE

Thorndike Press • Chivers Press
Thorndike, Maine USA   Bath, England

This Large Print edition is published by Thorndike Press, USA and by Chivers Press, England.

Published in 2000 in the U.S. by arrangement with Golden West Literary Agency.

Published in 2000 in the U.K. by arrangement with Golden West Literary Agency.

U.S. Hardcover 0-7862-2276-X (Western Series Collection)
U.K. Hardcover 0-7540-4025-9 (Chivers Large Print)
U.K. Softcover 0-7540-4026-7 (Camden Large Print)

The text of this Large Print edition is unabridged.
Other aspects of the book may vary from the original edition.

Set in 16 pt. Plantin.

Printed in the United States on permanent paper.

British Library Cataloguing in Publication Data available

Library of Congress Cataloging-in-Publication Data

Frazee, Steve, 1909–
    Cry, coyote / Steve Frazee.
        p. (lg. print) cm.
    ISBN 0-7862-2276-X (lg. print : hc : alk. paper)
    1. Large type books.   I. Title.
PS3556.R358 C79 2000
    813´.54—dc21   99-048282

Cry, Coyote

Chapter 1

The town of Nelson, Belknap County, Colorado, was baking under the weight of the hottest summer John Sexton could remember. At the lower end of the street a diamond-stacked engine waiting to help the westbound over the Madero Range gasped like a dying monster, attended by a few loafers who looked like melting lumps against the shady side of the station.

Sexton's lathered sorrel was the only horse in sight. It lowered its head and made a weary blowing sound after he leaped down and ran across the slatted walk into McRae's pharmacy.

"Doc! Doc!" The tiny front room with its counter and bottles on shelves was empty. And there was no one in back, either, where McRae had his meager hospital equipment.

"Doc!" Sexton started to run up the narrow steps to McRae's living quarters. Sunshine through an upstairs window showed dust motes dancing in the air, and the passage was thick with heat and the resinous odor of drying boards. There was no answer.

"Christ!" Sexton cried. He went outside and ran toward Glinkman's Sundown saloon. His heavy boots touched the walk lightly. He was a farmer, but he moved with the controlled grace of an athlete.

His face verged on gauntness, the flesh knit to strong facial bones with little waste of contour. His upper lip was short, his jaw strong without false thrust or bulldog bluntness. Sandy beard stubble held the caked dust of his riding. His eyes were brown, intense now with his urgency.

He burst into the Sundown and yelled, "Where's Doc McRae?"

Lew Glinkman's silvery head rose from behind the bar where he had been tinkering with something. His hair was parted in the middle, two great wings above a long, narrow face with the pale, unblemished skin common to nuns.

"Ain't he in his office, John?"

"No!" Sexton looked around as if to find better counsel. He and Glinkman were the only people in the room.

"I thought he might be back. He rode out to Champe's place last night. A shooting. Champe cracked down on another one of those bums he hires —" Glinkman saw he was wasting breath. "He'll be here soon."

"How soon?"

"Well, I can't say exactly." Glinkman drew a beer and wiped the foam with an ivory blade. "Have one while you're waiting, John. This damned run of heat —"

"It's my girl, Lew. Mary. She's got an awful fever. At first we thought — He wouldn't be in the hotel, would he?"

Glinkman glanced across the street at the Sawatch House. "I would have seen him go in. He could have swung back by way of Belknap's ranch. One of Frank's girls had the summer complaint, or something. He could have —"

Sexton started toward the door.

"Wait a minute, now! No use to wear yourself out in the heat before you know. He was going to pull some teeth for Pete Renwick this afternoon. Pete came dragging in late last night, but Doc had to go to the Five Bar, so he said he'd do it today. The chances are he'll be here any minute."

Sexton walked back to the bar. He took off his hat and wiped his forehead with his sleeve. Two triangular patches of scalp where his hair was thinning appeared almost white against the hard tan of his face. Damp with sweat, his hair stood bristly and sandy farther back on his head.

"Of all the times Jim Champe has to pick to get into one of his shooting scrapes! Damn him! Any other time —"

"Those things just happen, John," Glinkman said. He glanced at the beer which Sexton had not noticed. "Kids can get awful sick, you know, and then the next day —"

"You haven't got any kids, Lew." Sexton spun away from the bar. He went out on the run, crossed the street and leaped up the steps of the Sawatch House. A few minutes later he returned. "He isn't there. Pete says he's supposed to be back."

"He'll be here, John."

"She's never had anything but measles. It's that fever that worries Moira and me. It burns your hand just to touch her."

Sexton turned his back to the bar, watching the street. Sweat and dust had made a gray edge on his shirt collar. He needed a haircut. The dark skin of his neck was like his face, without wrinkles or looseness. He stood quietly, but the tension came from him like heat from a stove.

"My damned sink plugged up again," Glinkman said. "It drains out into the alley and —"

"Just that one time with measles. Damn Jim Champe anyway! Why'd he have to pick a time like this?"

"He didn't pick it, John. You know —"

"I can't wait. I'll ride back past Belknap's."

"You might miss him."

"If I meet him I'll save an hour or so. That might make a world of difference. If he comes back here, send him right out, Lew. Tell him —"

"I'll leave word with Crowley before I ride out toward Champe's. That way we'll have a double chance to save time." Glinkman took his apron off.

"You're a white man, Lew." Sexton spoke with the simple wonder of the self-sufficient man who never asks for help. The intensity of his look embarrassed Glinkman, and then Sexton ran out.

Without thinking, Glinkman poured the glass of beer into the sink. The stopped drain growled at him, and the beer spread out on the tin bottom. Glinkman cursed. He locked up and went to get a horse from Crowley's livery.

The train was grinding in when Sexton rode away. A layer of acrid smoke and heat rushed down the street at him. Against his judgment, not wanting to waste time to

11

change horses, he sent the sorrel out of town on the trot, into the flats where heat was scorching a turpentine odor from the sage.

The hot press of the sun was on him, and the dust he left behind him hung in the air like limp flags. The sage flats swept up to mesas of piñon and juniper. His own place was off to his right, up toward the head of Agate Valley. He was going now northwest, toward Frank Belknap's K, hurried by the memory of the worry in Moira's eyes.

He knew he was pushing the sorrel too hard, but it would last to the K. He searched ahead for dust. A stifling, motionless land looked back at him, piñons and junipers on broken hills. Far beyond, the serrated crests of the Sawatch Range ripped a pale blue sky.

The streaks of snow up there were mockery to a man coated with dust and itching with sweat. At Cow Creek he let the sorrel drink, and then put the horse into the hard lift to the aspen belt.

Belknap's place was at the head of long meadows. Less a few hundred tons, he raised enough hay here to serve his own needs, for this was a country of mild winters and the great upland meadows on the skirts of the Sawatch held his cattle well enough the year around.

The house was a tremendous structure, half stone and half logs. Rusty Nichols, one of Belknap's riders, had said there was more glass in it than in all the saloons of the county. There was an oldness and a solidity about the place that rounded out the fact that old Scott Belknap had settled here in Indian days.

And the fine state of repair said that Belknaps would be here for generations to come.

The big front door was closed. Sexton leaped down and ran toward the house.

"Ain't no one there, Sexton." Linneus Carrothers came from the trees at the side of the house, his grizzled hair on end, his face sour; it was obvious that he had been asleep back in the shade where the Belknap girls had a summer house with hammocks.

"I'm looking for the doctor. I heard one of Frank's kids was sick —"

"Harriet was sick. She's all right now. They went up to Meldrum Park to get out of the heat."

Sexton went back across the yard and pulled the sorrel away from a watering trough. "If McRae comes by tell him we need him bad at my place."

Carrothers yawned. "I'll tell him."

"I need a fresh horse."

"They're mostly in the summer camps."

"One is enough."

"I'm just a flunky here," Carrothers said. "Belknap might say I had no right to loan his horses." There was a sour stream of self-pity in his voice, and at the same time, superiority.

"I know what Frank would say. I need a horse."

"Frank ain't exactly like his father. I got along with old Scott all right, but say I loan you a horse now and Frank comes back and says I got no right to do it. He gives me hell, say, and then . . ."

Sexton listened no longer. He slopped water on his face at the trough. He drank from cupped hands. He could take a horse and the whining old man could go to hell, but pride and anger held Sexton back. He went up in the saddle and felt the ragged stiffening of the sorrel against his weight.

"A while ago I seen somebody riding toward town off to the east, if that's any help," Carrothers said. "I ain't saying it was McRae, but maybe —"

"How long ago?"

"Just before I tried to get some rest. Ten

minutes maybe. Then you woke me up —"

Sexton was riding away. It could be McRae. He might have swung up to Meldrum Park after leaving Jim Champe's place.

From the first high ridge east of the K he saw two riders. Foam was splashing from the mouth of the sorrel when he came within hailing distance of the men. The riders swung around, dismounting by a knob of rock on top of a hill. Sexton knew that neither was McRae. They were the Stalcup brothers, Irv and Will, who owned the Circle Arrow, northeast over Mexican Ridge from Sexton's farm.

The sorrel labored up the hill and stopped, trembling. "Have you seen Doc McRae?" Sexton asked.

The attitude of the Stalcups was stiff. They considered the question as if it were a trick. They looked like men expecting trouble.

Will shook his head. "Haven't seen him, Sexton." It would be Will who spoke. He was the civil one, a heavy, bold-nosed man with bulging gray eyes. He wore broadcloth where Irv wore faded denim.

Irv Stalcup was a burly chunk of man. The sun had chipped his face into scabby patches. His eyes were small and contentious, and his lips twisted close to his teeth when he talked. He was still on guard about something.

"What's the trouble, Sexton?" Will asked.

"Sick girl."

"Oh? That's too bad." Will glanced at his brother. "If we see McRae in town, we'll sure as hell send him out, won't we, Irv?"

Irv did not bother to answer. He said, "You've damned near ruined that sorrel, Sexton."

"I know it, but now I've got to get home and then maybe I'll have to ride toward the Five Bar."

Irv said, "Before you start all that, you'd better go to the K and get another horse."

This blank refusal of a question Sexton had not asked embarrassed Will. He looked away from Sexton. He wiped his face with a red bandana laid loosely around his neck to prevent sweat from soiling his coat collar. "By God, it's been a hot summer."

Mary was tossing in a hot room with a fever eating her. She was seven. She had her mother's beauty. Sexton's pride could not stand, even against refusal. He had made a mistake in Nelson. He had let

16

pride and anger keep him from taking a horse at the K, but now there was only urgency left.

He looked at Irv. "If one of you will switch with me, I'll leave your horse on the creek at Lindstrom's. I can get one from him." It was only a few miles out of their way.

"We're going to town," Irv said. "You came from the K, didn't you? Why didn't you get a fresh horse there?"

Sexton looked at Will. "Well, I don't know," Will said reluctantly. He glanced at his brother.

"I've got a sick girl," Sexton said. "By God, don't you understand that?"

"Sure, sure." Will was still looking to his brother for an answer. Irv was studying Sexton with the contempt of a strong man for a weak man who had to beg for something.

Sexton ground his anger back. "Will one of you ride to Lindstrom's, then, and tell him to send one of his boys to my place to tell my oldest boy to look for McRae on the trail to Champe's?"

"You don't even know where the doctor is." Will spread his hands helplessly.

Irv turned away abruptly. He walked to his horse and mounted. "Come on, Will.

17

We'd be fools to go near that crazy Swede right now."

"That's a fact, Sexton." Will tried to cover shame by adding quickly: "We'll send Doc right out if we find him in town, Sexton. Maybe the girl will be all right anyway. I sure hope so."

Sexton watched the Stalcups ride away. A terrible feeling of personal failure dragged through him.

He had to leave the sorrel a mile from Lindstrom's farm. He stripped the rig and laid it in the grass and gave the spraddle-legged animal one moment of pity before he started at a fast walk toward the creek. It was no cooler here in the lower part of Agate Valley than it had been in town.

Donn Lindstrom ran out to meet him when Sexton was two hundred yards from the buildings. Long-boned, red-faced, Lindstrom was waving a rifle. He was panting as if he would burst, and his lips flipped saliva as he shouted: "John! I was ready to shoot you! I am ready to shoot somebody!"

Sweat was burning Sexton's eyes. Lindstrom was shaking the rifle in his face like a finger. "Let's see the gun, Donn."

"The river! The Stalcups killed our river!"

"That's bad. Let's see that rifle, Donn." Sexton pushed the muzzle aside when Lindstrom thrust it at him. He took the piece and let the hammer down to safety; then he shook the sweat from his face and cleared the fur from his mouth, standing a moment drunk with fatigue and worry. "Has Doc McRae been past here?"

"By the dam on Mexican Ridge, that's how they did it! Bill Nafinger knows. The Stalcups, John! No water in the river!" Incoherent, wild, Lindstrom reached out to grab the rifle.

Sexton pushed him back. "We'll have to see about it, Donn. Has McRae ridden by?"

"No! I am talking about the river! They —"

"We'll take care of that." Sexton led the way toward the house. "I've got to find the doctor."

Lindstrom's pale blue eyes were bloodshot with rage and heat. He began to gain control of himself. "Who is sick?"

"My girl."

"I am sorry." In the same breath Lindstrom added: "They killed the water. I was ready to shoot somebody. I thought you might be a Stalcup."

"I need a horse, Donn."

"Yes! All of us will go up there, with

plows, with shovels, with —"

"In a day or two."

Mrs. Lindstrom and two of her younger girls were standing in the yard. Sexton gave her the rifle and saw the relief in her eyes, followed immediately by a glance of sympathy. "We heard, John. Cabot rode here looking for you to be coming back." She slid the rifle behind her long gray skirts.

The Lindstrom boys were standing at the creek. One of them yelled, "It's getting lower, Pa!"

Lindstrom went into a new burst of excitement, cutting the air with his hands.

"Donn! Donn!" his wife shouted. "Get the horse for Mr. Sexton!" Her husband paid no attention until she repeated the command in Swedish.

Sexton pounded away on a big-bellied, unshod gray. Agate Valley was shaped like a champagne bottle, Lindstrom holding the narrow lower end of it, with his fields edging against sage hills. The Renault farm was next and then the Nafinger place, and at the head, where the creek made slow S turns through rich deep soil, lay Sexton's 640 acres.

He splashed across the creek below the Renault bridge, veering toward the road. Sam Renault was standing on the rickety bridge, a blocky little man with a black spade beard. He waved Sexton on.

The gate at the north end of the farm reflected the condition of the whole place. It sagged, and was held by a mass of rusty wire that was hard to untangle.

Sexton had to go close to the Nafinger house. The big-bellied horse was blowing hard, so he stopped to loosen the cinch and let the animal catch its wind. Mrs. Nafinger met him, a small, intense, red-haired woman.

"Have you got him located yet?" she asked.

"Not yet. Did Cabot say how Mary was when he came by here?"

"He didn't stop that long." Mrs. Nafinger pressed a small bottle of black fluid into Sexton's hand. "Tell Moira to try this: two teaspoons every hour. It helps my kids."

"Thanks, Sue."

The woman glanced toward the creek. "I suppose Lindstrom told you?"

Sexton nodded, watching the horse.

"Bill went to town to talk to Judge Crowley. They have no right to the water, have they?"

"None at all." Sexton found a damp bandana in his hip pocket. He wiped his face. "Have any of your kids ever had a real bad fever, Sue?"

"Several times. They're still alive." Sue Nafinger gave Sexton a quiet smile of confidence. "Two teaspoons every hour, remember, if Moira wants to try it before the doctor gets there."

Sexton felt better when he left. Sue Nafinger watched him pound away, and then her face lost the confidence she had held out to him. She ran into the house and picked her baby from the cradle and held it tightly.

Crossing his own land, Sexton rode beside haystacks that were dark with age. This was the finest land on the creek. Native grasses stood high, prime, ready for cutting any time. Cabot, his oldest boy, was on the roof of Mary's room, drenching the shingles with a bucket of water. He tossed the bucket down to Malcolm, the youngest son, who filled it from a barrel on a stone boat a horse had dragged from the creek. Then Malcolm passed the bucket up to Roman, who was halfway up a ladder to the roof.

All the brothers had their father's sandy hair. They watched him rush into the yard, not stopping in their work. Cabot called softly, "Did you find him?"

"He's probably at Champe's ranch. How is she?"

After a moment Cabot said, "Not very good."

Malcolm spilled a bucket of water he was dragging from the barrel. He began to cry all at once but he dipped the bucket back into the barrel and carried it over to the ladder.

Sexton went quietly into the sickroom. His wife was bent over the bed, putting damp towels on the child's body. Moira Sexton did not look around when she asked, "How soon will he be here?"

"I —" Sexton's breath came out in a long sigh. "I have to go on over to Champe's. I think he's there."

Moira looked at him then, a question, and behind that, for an instant, panic. It rocked him like a tremendous blow on a nerve center. It left him weak and loose inside, for when fear broke through the endless layers of Moira Sexton's courage it shattered one of the strong foundations of her husband's life.

"How is she now? Is it worse?"

"We need the doctor," Moira said. She gathered the tough fibers of her strength to give her husband a faint smile. "It can't be diphtheria or scarlet fever. She has no sore throat, or hasn't all along. I know it isn't typhoid."

She was a tall woman, with the dark and white coloring of her Irish ancestry. Her hair was raven black, her eyes a searching green. She was the most beautiful woman Sexton had ever cared to see.

Water spilled from the roof. Cabot was trying to move as quietly as he could up there. Malcolm's voice came through the open window. "We'll have to go back to the creek for another load."

Mary rolled her head from side to side. She tossed her arms aimlessly, small arms that were scarlet with the grip of fever. Moira lifted a damp towel from her chest and dipped it into a pan beside the bed. Sexton knew he had to go, but he stayed another minute.

He put two fingers gently on Mary's forehead. "Still burning up," he muttered. Mary's hair was like her mother's. Soft and fine it lay against her temple cups, then fell in two black braids against the hot pillow. Four days ago she had raced like a sprite after her brothers along the creek bank. The memory of her laughter trailed across Sexton's mind like a knife cutting him.

"I'll go on now to Champe's."

"Send Cabot." Moira did not look at him, but he felt the same conveyence of brief panic that had come from her eyes.

24

Sexton remembered the medicine then. He took it from his pocket. "Sue Nafinger gave me this. She said —"

"God bless her, but it might choke her now, John. The best I can do is dribble water into her mouth."

Sexton set the bottle carefully on a chair. He picked it up immediately, wiped a smudge of dust from it, and put it back upon the chair. "I'll send Cabot."

Cabot was sixteen. He was already as tall as his father.His eyes were deep-set, his mouth thinner than any of the Sextons'. Looking at him, Sexton remembered that Cabot had never teased his sister as younger brothers had.

The boy heard his father's orders and nodded. In two minutes he was racing away bareback on his pony. It was ten miles to the Champe ranch. Sexton figured the hours and was afraid. He watched Roman and Malcolm dipping water at the creek, and he heard Malcolm say, "Now it's almost quit running altogether."

Sexton unsaddled Lindstrom's horse and put it into the corral. He went inside once more. "How is she now?"

"The same."

He stared at his daughter. He was a man who had never asked any quarter from life.

25

He asked it now, and then he said, "Let me clean up a little and then maybe you can rest."

He washed in the kitchen, soaping away sweat and dust and leather stains from his hands, sloshing water on the spare planes of his face. His hands were big and powerful. He flexed them, wishing there was some way he could use them to grapple with the shadow in the sickroom. Between movements of the towel against his face he looked out on the long run of his hayland. There was enough grass in sight to make more hay than the whole country had need of.

The splash of water on the roof went on all afternoon. At intervals Sexton went out to scan the country north toward Mexican Ridge. *Maybe I should have gone myself.* But he knew that he could not have ridden as fast as Cabot.

Sexton and his wife put their wills solidly against the menace in the sickroom, and in doing so they achieved a closeness that was almost perfect.

The sun was dying when Mary began to cry out in a frightened tone, "Mommie? Mommie?" She searched the mists plaintively, and Moira answered over and over, smiling, holding the small hands, until at last the child relaxed.

It seemed to Sexton then that she was breathing easier. The terror flickering in his mind began to subside, but it needed only a touch, an uneven spacing in Mary's shallow breathing, to flare up again.

With the going of the sun a small breeze ran across the fields of tall grass and the first breath of evening coolness flowed into the room.

Moira wiped her face and hands on a piece of white sheeting. "Tell the boys to get themselves something to eat."

The yard was muddy from water that had spilled off the roof. Sexton told his sons they had done enough. They leaned against the barrel wearily, staring at him.

"She's better, we think. You kids get something to eat."

He unhitched the horse from the stone boat while the boys were stumbling into the kitchen. Unharnessing in the barn, he heard the sound of hoofbeats in the north. He ran outside and saw Cabot's little pinto and McRae's big red roan coming through the upper pasture gate.

"Moira! The doctor's here!"

McRae's shirt was rolled high on his thick brown arms. He dismounted in a leap and reached for the tie strings behind the saddle.

"I'll get the bag!" Sexton said. He untied the doctor's coat and his grip while McRae was going inside.

Sexton and his wife stood close together and watched McRae in the sickroom. He was deft with his hands, slow with his opinion. For thirty years he had practiced medicine, and now his brown beard was sprinkled with gray. He was thorough with his examination. Sexton felt confidence now from the shifting of a burden.

"How long has she been completely out of her head?" McRae asked. His voice was deep and even.

"About an hour after John left this morning — about eight o'clock."

Not looking at the parents, McRae asked several more questions. At length he looked directly at Sexton and Moira, studying them as if he were weighing one against the other to determine which had the greater stability. He settled on Moira. "She has scarlet fever."

"Her throat was never sore!" Moira said.

"That happens sometimes with scarlet fever." McRae glanced at Sexton. "How about some coffee, John?" The flesh around the doctor's eyes was smudged with fatigue.

"How bad is it?" Sexton asked.

McRae's sharp eyes touched Moira again. "She's very sick. I don't have to tell you that. I'd like some coffee, John."

Moira nodded at her husband. Sexton went into the kitchen. His hands were clumsy. Nothing seemed to be in place as he built a fire and started coffee. Malcolm and the other two boys were eating radish sandwiches.

"What did he say?" Cabot asked.

"He said she was pretty sick."

The three boys watched Sexton uneasily as he kept lifting the stove lid to hurry a fire that was barely kindled. Suddenly, in the middle of a bite, Malcolm's mouth twisted and he began to cry. He threw his sandwich toward the woodbox and ran out of the room.

"He was already started here," Cabot said. "Lew Glinkman rode all the way to Champe's to tell him. I only had to go as far as Mexican Creek."

Roman said, "The Stalcups made a gouge and a dam and turned all the Agate water down Mexican Creek."

"You didn't see it!" Cabot said. "I told you about it, just now."

"Let's not have a fight over it." Sexton listened to the murmur of voices in the sickroom. Though he knew he was of no use there, he was uneasy about the way the doctor had sized him up and got him out of the room.

"Lindstrom was as sore as a bull with a boil," Cabot said. "He was running around like a crazy man, waving a rifle. He said —"

"Be quiet, Cabot." A sudden silence in the other part of the house worked on Sexton. He had turned away from the stove and headed toward the living-room door when he heard McRae say:

"Yes, that was a good thing to do. I'd say it helped." The deep, even voice held no undertone of worry, Sexton decided. He tried to build his own hope on it.

The boys went outside to find Malcolm, and Sexton heard them calling his name. He realized that it was growing dark when he found himself concentrating on the leaks of light coming from the stove. He could see the yellow patch on the floor of the living room and he knew that Moira had lighted a lamp.

He kept lifting the lid of the coffeepot, waiting for the sound of boiling.

The voices in the sickroom stopped suddenly. He heard the scrape of a chair. The tenseness in him was like a steel rod. A shadow blotted out the light coming from the bedroom. Moira said, "John." Her voice was under control, but there was a tone in it that stopped Sexton's breath. He ran.

Mary was in convulsions. Sexton knew that a lifetime would not be enough to forget the small hands clutching at the sheet, the jerking, the whole protest against finality.

When McRae straightened up at last his arms fell slackly at his sides. He looked at Sexton and Moira with an understanding that spoke of his own three children dead long ago of typhoid, and with an understanding of parents bereft since time began. And then he looked beyond them, and his pouched eyes were bitter with this defeat and the memories of old defeats and the certainty of future losses. He straightened his heavy shoulders. He met the moment and the future without falseness. "Go on out. I'll tell you when to come back."

Sexton stared at McRae, hating him for an instant because the doctor was the most available linkage to a black event.

"Go on out." McRae was brutally tired, but the will to go on was there.

"Come on, John." Moira seemed to be without emotion. She led her husband from the room, but when they were outside her body went loose. "Mary," she sobbed, and crumpled against Sexton. He picked her up and carried her to their bedroom and sat beside her, holding tightly to her hand while she wept.

Air from the cooling land made ghostly movements against the white curtains. Sexton stared into the night, trying to drive away remembrance of the last fifteen minutes. He relived the day, his futile ride, his arguments with faces that were evil now, his hurrying on foot across Lindstrom's barley field after the sorrel gave out.

Every moment that he had been delayed raked him with barbed claws.

Moria stopped crying. "Where are the boys?"

"Outside somewhere."

"We'd better tell them now."

Sexton rose. "I'll go do it."

She held to his hand after he was on his feet. "We didn't fail. We did the best we knew how."

"I suppose. I know you did. McRae too." Sexton started out. His voice was numbed with bitterness. "And it's all no consolation whatever. She died."

He went into the yard. Coyotes on the hills were crying too, a haunting song of all things lost down through the ages.

Chapter 2

Before sunrise Sexton walked alone beside the creek above the house. Already the gathering stickiness of the air foretold another hot day. Without humor he remembered Lindstrom's excited talk. *They killed our river!* Trout were dying in the quiet pools, flashing erratically, showing their white undersides as they strove to keep from rolling on their backs.

He turned away from the sight quickly.

His long acres of hay gave him no satisfaction. The deep soil cut by the river meant nothing this morning. Deep in him was the magic of the earth, the love of working the earth and watching the fruitfulness of it, but today the farm was failure.

McRae rode out from the barn. A night's rest had taken the pouches from his eyes. The vitality of him seemed tremendous as he looked down quietly at Sexton and said, "I told Moira I'd tell the folks down the creek on my way to town."

Sexton nodded. "Thanks, Doc."

McRae studied the creek. "That won't hurt you much at this time of year, will it?"

"No. Irv will turn the water back when he gets tired of playing." Sexton broke the seed top from a blade of grass. "If we could have reached you sooner —"

"We can't go back, John. What are the Stalcups doing, watering their patch of hay on Lower Mexican?"

"I suppose." Sexton had lost time overtaking the Stalcups, more time because they would not switch one of their horses for his. "If we could have hurried things a little more, Doc — say, an hour —"

"It would have made no difference, I'm afraid." McRae pointed toward the creek. "You've got the oldest decree in this part of the country, haven't you?"

"Nine feet. It went with the place when I bought it four years ago. You knew it was too late when you walked into the room, didn't you?"

McRae looked at Sexton angrily. "I never know that."

"But it's so. You told Moira after you sent me out to make coffee."

"Did your wife tell you I did?"

"No."

34

"It's true. I told her the chances were against us."

"Why didn't you tell me?"

"Because," McRae said, "she could take it better than you."

Sexton flipped the seed top away. He took a deep breath. "That's right."

"What are you trying to get at, John?"

"I don't know." Sexton shook his head. "I only wish we could have got you sooner."

"I've lost children to that kind of scarlet fever even when I was there early."

"What was the trouble at Champe's?"

"A shooting. Champe fired a man. They argued over his wages. Champe shot him."

"Will he live?"

McRae hesitated. "Maybe. I sent him to town this afternoon to go to the hospital in Cottonwood. Maybe he'll live."

"Champe owed him the money, didn't he?"

"I don't know," McRae said. "The cause of shootings is generally no concern of mine." McRae dismounted and walked over to Sexton. "Look, John, if I hadn't been at the Five Bar, I might have been farther away. Blame Mary's death on the fact that we have no medicine or knowl-edge to control scarlet fever."

"If Jim Champe hadn't shot a man because he's too Goddamn' crooked to pay what he owed, you'd have been in Nelson pulling Pete Renwick's teeth. I would have got you right away and maybe —"

"You don't know, John. I might have been fishing. I might have been clear up in the park with the Belknaps, checking up on Harriet. She's been sick —"

"She got well," Sexton said.

McRae studied Sexton with a troubled expression. He got back on his red roan. "When are you going to cut the hay?"

"Any time, I guess."

"Is the market for baled hay any better than it was last year?"

"No. I don't have a baler, either."

"You spoke of going over to oats in a lot of this valley."

"It takes time," Sexton said. "I'll get to it. Doc, if we could have reached you —"

"If I had been here two days ago, I can't say for sure that things would be any different. I've told Moira to watch the boys carefully. One of them may come down with it. Until that danger is past, I won't be any farther away than Nelson."

Sexton's face was bleak, his eyes bitter as he looked toward the hills. "I've got three boys, McRae. I had only one girl, and she made a singing inside of me whenever I looked at her."

Shock stood an instant in McRae's eyes. He turned his horse. "Start cutting the hay, John, as soon as you can. Work at it until you drop, hear me?"

The doctor rode away. Sexton saw him take off his coat before he was a hundred yards down the creek.

McRae was right, Sexton thought. There was nothing to be made of the time element. Lew Glinkman, leaving his business, had ridden all the way to the Champe place. Before, he had been another man to meet casually in town; now he was a friend that Sexton would never forget.

Sexton walked back to the corner of his corral. He was a logical man who had farmed most of his life. The elements had beaten him time and again, but he had never cursed them.

He had accepted all things with patience. And that was the way he must take this blow, he knew.

But it would not straighten out in his mind. He remembered Linneus Carrothers, whining about his inability to lend a horse; and Irvin Stalcup had not even considered helping. His brother Will, because he had been swayed away when he wanted to do a decent act, was more contemptible than Irv. Though Sexton could not blame them for his loss, neither could he forget them.

He wonderful, too, just what Frank Belknap's reaction would have been if Sexton had borrowed one of his horses over the objections of his flunky.

Now I'm really going out of my way to torture myself, he thought.

He watched the boys carrying furniture into the yard, scurrying to their mother's quiet orders. Moira was giving the house a cleaning, hurling her energy into work instead of thought. The women from down the creek would be here before long, and they would chide Moira for not waiting for their help; and yet any of them would have done as she was doing now.

The sun rose and the day was instantly oppressive. Vapor began to rise from the mud below the eaves of the room where Mary was. Sexton walked away from the corral, going past his machinery shed. He stopped to look at his mower. It was in good condition; he had sharpened the knives and greased the machine and tightened all loose bolts and parts the week before.

The mower was no longer a tool; it was futility.

He walked away and leaned on a fence, looking toward the mountains. It was cool up there. When the weather became too hot and bothered one of Belknap's girls, he took his family to their summer camp, worrying about nothing.

Sexton looked at his land, good land, the largest piece of the earth he had ever owned. This was his fourth place, but he had never moved from sheer aimlessness or because of failure. When he and Moira had brought the children here, they both had known that this was where they wanted to stay for good. The soil, the slow splashing of the creek, and the warm, productive summers had made a poetry of living. And there was always the mighty range to look upon, a sight to whet the spirit when toil dragged the body into weariness.

Today the earth was like earth in a thousand places; the river was dead, the heat was unbearable, and somewhere in the great mountains a devil's orchestra was playing thin music into John Sexton's ears.

There was no security in the world.

Presently Moira came to stand beside him. Her eyes were tired, but they were looking at today clearly. The way she was holding her mouth made her lips look thin. Sexton observed a few gray strands in her hair. All this he had seen before, but now he saw it from an odd detachment.

She put her hand upon his shoulder, and he felt his muscles tighten at the touch. There was a loneliness in him that he did not wish to share with anyone.

Moira said, "While the boys are resting for a few minutes shall we go up on the hill and —"

"There's no hurry. One spot up there is like another." His curtness surprised him. He added, "The neighbors will feel slighted if I don't leave some of the work to them."

Moira studied him intently. "I suppose so." Her hand slid from his shoulder and she went back to the house, and then she was hard at work again. Sexton watched Malcolm empty a mop bucket. The boy's clothes were faded and patched, his clumsy shoes a pair of brogans passed down from Roman.

Cabot and Roman came out, arguing about whose turn it was to get the next bucket of water. For once they were not loud in their bickering. Sexton looked at them with the same detachment with which he had looked at his wife. Their clothes were like Malcolm's, their futures just as uncertain. For the first time in his life a powerful resentment against his lot sprang in Sexton, spiraling up from some source he did not fully comprehend.

He walked along the fence until he came to the first hill. The farm enlarged before his view: the hard-won ditches along the slopes, the laterals fingering out into the fields, the overabundance of stacks. The buildings were a neat cluster, settled nicely within the line of young trees that would be a windbreak in time. Down toward the Renault place Sexton's few acres of oats made a high, clean color.

Today Sexton found no satisfaction in the scene. He stopped on a level place that faced the grandeur of the mountains. Down a few feet he knew he would strike white sand and clean gravel; and afterward he would build a stout fence around the place and paint it white.

He returned to the farm for a pick and shovel. Cabot came toward him, eager to help.

"Don't bother him now, Cabot," Moira said. "Come here and help me."

Malcolm stared sidewise at the tools. His face crumpled and he ran to the barn. Cabot turned away.

Sexton went to work. Seven years old with laughter running beautifully. And now, stillness forever in the grit of the earth. Let Donn Lindstrom, who fancied himself as a preacher, give the reasons that he felt. Let him speak the old words which would be without meaning to Sexton.

John Sexton knew that the foulness and injustice of death could not be healed with words.

Sweat soaked him as he worked. After a long time, gasping in the still heat, he saw his neighbors coming up the valley.

He worked more furiously then; this was his task.

Chapter 3

Sexton barely heard Lindstrom's service. Once, with humorless inconsistency, he wondered if God understood a Swedish accent. Bill Nafinger had made the box of rough lumber, and the women had covered it with white cloth. White was the color of angel wings, Mrs. Renault said.

White was the color of the gravel, too, Sexton thought. When he left to drive his family down the hill, he knew he had not accepted this last act; he was still savagely opposed to it, even when his logical mind told him that he must obey.

The heat seemed worse today than the day before.

Everyone had brought food. The house was too full of it, and too filled with women talk, and all the children were fretting under a harsh restraint that had been laid down to them in advance. Sexton said the proper words to the women, and then started toward the machinery shed where the men were sitting in the shade.

He heard Mrs. Renault say: "I remember when I lost Marie back in Nebraska. It was a summer like this . . ."

The men went on talking when Sexton approached the shed. He sat down on a box of bolts and scrap iron.

Bill Nafinger was saying, "I talked to him about an hour" — he glanced at Sexton — "Judge Crowley, when I went to see him yesterday," Nafinger was a tall man with a broad frame that was mostly all width and little depth. "He said the Stalcups were clear wrong, and any court would have to say the same." He smiled. "Then he said not to get in a hurry, that things would probably work out."

Sam Renault grinned. "Sounds like Lew Glinkman."

"Glinkman's all right," Sexton said curtly.

The three men looked at him quickly.

"Sure he is," Nafinger said, nodding.

"It ain't as if we needed the water." Renault fingered his spade beard. "The hay is ready to make right now. Hell, as far as that goes, I've been using Sexton's water most of the summer."

"Me too," Lindstrom said. "My decree ain't so good when the water is low."

They were edging the lead around to

Sexton, he knew. His decree was the oldest on Agate Creek, calling for nine feet of water. He did not need that much, but it was to take. Those below him had later decrees, in varying amounts, and in dry years they would have suffered if he had chosen to take his full call from the stream.

Lindstrom said, "Yesterday I was ready to shoot somebody, you bet, but maybe —" He waited for Sexton.

"They don't need what they're taking," Nafinger said. "I told the judge nobody here ever tried to make a stink when they took a little water to irrigate that patch of timothy on the lower end of Mexican Creek."

They waited for Sexton to say something. He was silent, studying them, their clothes, their work-worn appearance. Nafinger's wide shoulders were stooped. Lindstrom's thatch of yellow hair had been crudely trimmed with scissors, leaving square edges around his ears and at the back. Renault was getting gray at the temples.

I'm just like them, Sexton thought. All at once he did not like the identification. There was a blackness in him that made him reject everything he had been; and it wound in some strange, twist-

45

ing manner back to what had happened to him yesterday.

Nafinger mopped his brow. He kicked a wheel on the mower. "You got that thing in good shape, John. I wish mine was half as good."

"I been working on it some," Sexton said.

Lindstrom said: "If they water their hay when they should, they don't need the whole river now. Did you tell the judge that, Bill?"

"Sure!" Nafinger said. "I told him everything. We got the law with us, no question. It just depends on how far we want to go." He looked at Sexton.

"Lawing costs money," Renault said. "Even when you know you're right."

Nobody was hurt, Sexton thought. The Stalcups would turn the water back into Agate Creek maybe today or tomorrow. He said, "I'll go talk to them."

Lindstrom nodded vigorously. "All of us!"

"I'm willing," Nafinger said, "but maybe —"

"I'll go alone." Sexton wished they'd shut up about it. "Irv is up to his old tricks, that's all, trying to pick a fight. When he sees he can't get one, his interest will be gone."

"Yesterday I would shoot him into being interested," Lindstrom said. "But my woman talked to me and now I am not so mad. Still, taking the whole river —"

"I'll take care of it," Sexton said.

The sharpness of his tone brought an exchange of looks. After a time Nafinger said, "Your oats were looking awful good when I came by today."

"They looked good yesterday, too," Renault said.

There was a short laugh, but it died uneasily when Sexton kept staring at the ground.

"Suppose we all switch over to grains, like John is starting to do." Renault scratched heat prickle on the back of his hand. "Then some of us might be short. I got a cousin in Oregon that's been wanting me to come out that way for a long time. I'm sort of getting in the mood."

"I got a cousin in Sweden," Lindstrom said, "but I ain't in the mood to go back there."

"I'm serious." Renault nodded. "Me and the wife been talking about it for quite a spell."

Nafinger frowned. "You funning, Sam?"

"No, I'm not. The trouble is, who's

going to give me fifteen hundred for the place?"

"Nobody." Nafinger grinned. "But I will buy that gray team if you give me five years to pay."

"I'll make you a good deal on the grays," Renault nodded. "Don't think I won't."

They searched Renault's face. Lindstrom said, "He's serious."

"I am. Breaking up hayland to plant grain is going to be a long, tough haul. On top of that, I haven't got a good water right. Suppose John here sells out someday to somebody that turns out to be a sonofabitch. Then we could scoop puddles for our water in a dry year."

"Don't worry about that, Renault," Sexton said.

"I'm just saying what could happen. The wife and me talked it over. I'm ready to sell."

One of Lindstrom's boys, glad to be released from the restraint of walking and talking quietly near the house, came racing to say that dinner was ready.

The shade had been hot enough. The sun, as the men tramped to the house, was scorching.

"Never saw a summer like it!" Nafinger complained.

The sight of food turned Sexton's stomach. The fact that others could eat disgusted him.

After the meal the neighbors were restless, anxious to return to chores undone, reluctant to make the first move lest they be considered not properly sympathetic.

Sexton thanked them all for coming. The women clustered around Moira for last expressions of sympathy. For a while, allowing himself to understand the full sincerity of his friends, Sexton was himself.

But when the wagons were going from sight down the creek, the emptiness and the blackness settled in him again.

"They were fine," Moira said.

Sexton nodded.

"Alice Renault said she and Sam have been considering moving to Oregon."

"Yeah."

Moira studied Sexton quietly. "We all feel the same way, John; but she's gone now, and the tomorrows will keep coming just as they always have."

"Yeah, I know." Sexton walked away, hatless in the sun, striding fast as if to outdistance his thoughts.

He found himself on the creek bank a half-mile from the house. The yellow gravel of the river bed had dried gray in the sun and there was a dead smell in the heavy air. He stood above a pool where some of the seep from the subflow of his farm was spilling into the creek. A hundred or more trout had congregated there, fighting for the freshness.

There were too many of them. The weaker ones were sliding on their sides, dipping, weaving crazily through the pool. Sexton watched them with terrible fascination. They jerked and fought and protested against dying. Then they spun slowly to the bottom. Their white undersides as they lay there were the color of the box that had gone into the ground.

Sexton felt a hot swelling rising in his very fibers. He had talked quietly about the stoppage of the water; it had been the least of his troubles. But now a rage against the Stalcups was choking him.

He went back to the barn, walking so fast that his family met him in the yard. Moira asked, "What's the matter?"

"The trout are dying in the creek!" It was an answer without sense. Sexton realized the fact after he spoke; but he knew where his answer came from.

Moira's face turned pale. One glance at her and Sexton knew that her intuition, based on keen knowledge of him, had led her down the devious trail to the truth. He was irritated that even she should know him so well, for it seemed to be a criticism of him.

She said, "So you're going to see the Stalcups?"

"Yes. After I smash their dam."

Moira surprised him when she said slowly: "That might be a good idea. How will you do it?"

"Get me the heavy bar from the shed, Cabot." Sexton strode into the barn. He was going toward the sorrel's stall when he remembered that the horse was not there. It was dead. Raving mad about the water, Lindstrom had not thought to go after it yesterday until after it had staggered to the creek below his house. He had, at least, hauled the rig up with him today.

Sexton saddled Cabot's pinto.

The boys came into the barn, Cabot carrying the bar. He said, "If we use the wagon —"

"No! Don't any of you dare follow me."

The boys were standing by their mother when Sexton rode away with the heavy bar athwart the saddle. It was an awkward weight. Long before he walked the sweating pony up Mexican Ridge, the bar had taken heat from the sun and was hot to the touch.

Now he was in aspen country, but the heat was still intolerable. He stayed on the ridge, which was the spine of the watershed between a few small creeks flowing east and the southward drainage of Agate Creek. The Stalcup ranch was straight ahead of him, the Champe place to his right. Together with Frank Belknap, the Stalcups and Jim Champe controlled almost all of the parkland range below the curving sweep of the Sawatch Mountains.

There were a few bobtail ranchers on to the east, but the lot of them did not own a thousand cows. Wasteland to the east of the little outfits and the inhospitable Madero Range to the west of the Stalcup ranch limited operations. There was no cattle empire here; the three main outfits ran altogether about fifteen thousand head.

Sexton bored straight ahead. The aspens became taller, more dense. He knew where the dam would be, not far below the falls of Agate Creek.

Fifty years before, when the only white men in the country were trappers, wandering Englishmen, and an occasional dragoon troop from distant Santa Fe, two Frenchmen had built a trading post near the big springs that were the headwaters of Mexican Creek.

They soon found out that the springs went almost dry in summer, and so the Frenchmen had their Mexican employees supply the post with water by ditching through the gentle swell of Mexican Ridge to Agate Creek — this after the traders lost three men to Utes, who traded first and then amused themselves by nestling in the dark timber on the west side of the ridge to stick arrows into water carriers.

Cleaned out, the old ditch had served the Stalcups when they needed water for the patch of hay they raised haphazardly on the lower meadows of Mexican Creek.

The seven-mile ride had shaken down some of Sexton's rage, but his determination was unchecked. He was carrying the bar like a lance in order to clear the trees.

He came to the site of the trading post. Though aspens covered it now, it still commanded a tremendous view of the lower country. It was, he thought, a better place for a house than Belknap's location.

He saw his water coursing away to the east. A broken scraper lay on the bank. It was possible that the Stalcups merely had intended to clean the ditch and had gone deeper than necessary, so that the scouring of a strong head of water had cut the loose overburden deeply enough to rob Agate Creek.

It was possible: give even Irv Stalcup his due. And then Sexton remembered that Irv had refused him help when he was desperate enough to beg for it. To hell with both the Stalcups and all their kind. They would never get another cubic inch of water from Agate Creek.

Sexton rode along the ditch until it led him to the dam in the black timber below the falls. It was cool there; the trees were mossy, high-reaching. The dam was simple, well made. They had dug into the banks on both sides of the stream, dropped trimmed trees into the slots to mace the initial barrier, and then had piled sacks of sand on the upstream side of the log wall. Over the bags the builders had placed tarpaulins, so that now scarcely any water was filtering through the dam.

It was simple to build, and it was even easier to wreck.

Sexton dropped his bar. He dismounted and picked up the tool. Moving deliberately, without haste, he found a short piece of timber to use as a pry block. He made ready to lever up one end of the top log across the stream.

The pistol shot was loud. A bullet ripped the log about a foot from the end of his bar. Sexton dropped flat. An instant later a man laughed.

"All right, Sexton; you can get up. I wasn't trying to hit you."

Stan Elwood, the Stalcups' foreman, was standing in the trees above the dam, a smoking pistol in his hand.

"Damn, that was funny," he said, and laughed again with genuine humor. He was a rangy man with a loose-skinned face that moved freely in all his expressions. It was said that he was the only man Irv Stalcup ever thought it worth while to be civil to.

Sexton's moment of panic was gone. "This dam is coming out."

"Not until Irv says so." Elwood was sure. His loyalty to Irv Stalcup was unquestionable.

"Where is Irv?"

"Still in town, I guess." Elwood walked along the creek bank, studying Sexton carefully. He put his pistol away. "I got orders to let 'er run until he comes back."

"You don't need that much water."

"Maybe not, but I got my orders." Elwood had never been a trouble-picking man. Several times on his way to town he had stopped at Sexton's place for a cup of coffee and a few minutes of idle talk. Sexton had liked him well enough then.

Today was different. Elwood stood across the creek, tough and sure of himself, carrying out the orders of a man for whom Sexton was building a grinding hatred.

Sexton waded the stream. Elwood backed off a few steps, standing with his hand on his pistol butt, weighing Sexton's intentions with cool gray eyes.

"No use for me and you to have any trouble about this," Elwood said. "But she runs until Irv says otherwise."

"It's not his water, not one drop of it."

"I ain't no lawyer, Sexton." Elwood was reasonable enough, but he was watchful, and his determination was like a rock.

There was a round-point shovel sticking in the ground. Automatically, Sexton took the handle and rested on it while water ran from his clothes into the mold.

"Irv might need more hay this winter than he has for a long time," Elwood said. "About fifteen years back, when he was just getting started, we had a summer like this, and the following winter was a bastard. It well nigh cleared Irv out."

Sexton kept working his hands on the weathered shovel handle. "Don't you figure Will owns any of the Circle Arrow?"

Elwood looked surprised. "Sure, both of them. Why'd you ask that?"

"Just wondered. How come Irv took the whole creek?"

"We didn't intend to, and then the dam went in so easy and Irv got to laughing about how —" Elwood stopped.

"About how we'd feel when we saw the river drying up. It sure was funny, Elwood. It's got to come out of there."

"That's up to Irv."

"Say we let just part of it back now, just enough to keep —"

"No, I can't do it, Sexton. Irv gave me orders. If he stays in town a week, I'm still following his word."

"The trout are dying." Sexton spoke quietly but there was a roiling inside him that was like a pain. He gripped the shovel hard.

"Hell, the country's full of fish. What's a few dead fish?"

Sexton wrenched the shovel from the ground and swung it in the same motion. It was a long reach, for Elwood had held off a few paces. He went back a step and reached for his pistol as Sexton took one long pace forward to make his blow carry.

The blade of the shovel clanged on Elwood's pistol as it came in front of him.

The pistol flew out of his hand and the shovel carried through to knock him back another step. Sexton dropped the tool and rushed in. He tried to win the fight with one blow into Elwood's stomach.

Elwood twisted. Sexton's fist struck the man's hip bone with an impact that almost numbed his arm. Both men were off balance then. Sexton slipped and had to put one hand down to keep from falling. Elwood clubbed him in the back of the neck. There was a grainy, rushing sound in Sexton's brain as he fell forward. He grabbed Elwood's ankles and jerked the man's legs from under him.

They fell apart from each other, Sexton on his hands and knees, Elwood catching himself with his hands as he drew his legs back to spring up.

They rose and faced each other. "The dam comes out," Sexton said. "If I have to kill you."

"You can try. That's all a steer can do." Elwood flipped blood away from the crotch of his thumb where the hammer spur of his pistol had cut. He moved into Sexton, striking him in the face with long, straight blows.

Sexton ducked and hammered at Elwood's stomach and chest. They were savages, not knowing or caring now about the reason for their efforts to kill each other. They poured their energy into a few brutal minutes and then they were almost done.

Sexton tried to stagger in, to get his hands on Elwood's throat. Elwood set himself and knocked Sexton on his back beside the shovel. The chemicals of savagery had poured too much stimulation into Sexton's blood to let him go out with one sharp blow.

He lay groggily beside the shovel, seeing the weariness in Elwood, watching the man's arms drop at his sides. "This is about enough," Elwood muttered. He started over to pick up his pistol.

Sexton got both hands on the shovel. He rolled over and came to his feet, knees bent and shaking. From the end of the long handle he whirled the shovel in a hissing arc, intending to crack Elwood's hand as it touched the pistol.

Elwood saw the motion. He jerked his hand back and pulled his body out of danger. His right foot was close to the pistol. The edge of the shovel came down on the instep. It cut through the boot and stuck for an instant before it fell away. Elwood groaned. He sat down, his face shocked white.

Blood poured from the slice in his boot. He stared at it. "Jesus Christ, Sexton!"

Sexton started to pick up the pistol. He fell on his hands and knees but he got hold of the weapon and threw it into the creek. "Now, by God," he said.

Elwood was not interested. Staring at the mass of blood pouring from his boot, he settled back slowly and passed out.

"You're not hurt, damn you!"

His mouth half open, Elwood lay as if dead. Sexton shook him. "Quit faking, Elwood!"

The man did not stir.

With fumbling movements that burned his tired arms Sexton ripped his shirt off and started to bind it around Elwood's foot, over boot and all. He stopped when he realized what he was doing. The creek was icy. He stood knee deep in it and threw water all over himself. His mind was much clearer when he went back to Elwood.

He pulled the boot off. The sock came with it, except fragments of cloth which were sliced into the wound. Elwood's foot was cut almost half in two. *I did that,* Sexton thought with a strange sense of wonder. He plucked at the shreds of sock. He poured a hatful of water on the foot.

The bleeding did not abate.

Grabbing the man by his good leg, Sexton dragged him to the creek and let the injured foot dangle in the water. Elwood opened his eyes and sighed. Sexton watched blood swirling away and knew the cold was not helping. He twisted Elwood around until the foreman was lying on the bank, and then Sexton removed his own shirt and bound it tightly around the wound.

"You didn't have to cut my foot off, Sexton."

"To hell with you. You tried to kill me."

"No. I was only going to —"

"Where's your horse?"

Elwood pointed toward the black timber.

Sexton found the horse munching loose hay near a makeshift camp that could not be seen from the dam. He tore down the canvas shelter, kicked cooking utensils into the brush, and then saddled the horse and led it back to Elwood.

"How bad is the foot, Sexton? It feels —"

"McRae can fix it." McRae had not been able to do anything about Mary. "Stay right there," Sexton added.

He waded the creek and went to work with the bar. He pried up logs. He punctured the canvas face with the bar and drove the tool into sacks of earth, and then the water worked with him. Agate Creek was running once more in its natural channel. Let Donn Lindstrom go in circles and shout about it.

Sexton went back to Elwood. "I'll take you to town now. Get up."

Elwood rode with his feet hanging loose beside the stirrups. Because the bandage was soaked and coming loose before they were off Mexican Ridge, Sexton used Elwood's shirt to bind up the foot again.

"I don't know why I keeled over." Elwood was almost apologetic. A while later there was terror in his voice. "The flies are trying to get into it, Sexton!"

Sexton got down again. "They can't. Doc McRae will fix it up."

When they rode into Sexton's yard, Elwood was weaving. He started to fall out of the saddle. Moira and Cabot tried to catch him, and all three of them crashed to the ground.

Sexton and Cabot carried the injured man into the kitchen, and Moira went to work on the foot.

Cabot took one look and said, "My God, Dad —"

"Watch your language." Moira gave her

son a sharp look. "Go get the wagon ready."

Elwood came to. "I don't want no wagon. I ain't going into town in the back of no wagon. How bad is it, Mrs. Sexton?"

"You'll be all right, Mr. Elwood. Don't worry."

"I ain't going into town in no wagon."

"You'll ride, then," Sexton said.

Moira did a good job of bandaging. She gave her husband some extra cloth. When Elwood was back on his horse, she stood looking at Sexton so quietly that he said: "You told me it would be a good idea! The water is back in the creek!"

"Yes, I guess I said that." The searching, calm appraisal did not change. "Take him on in to the doctor."

"I ought to go along," Cabot said. "Maybe the Stalcups —"

"You stay here!" Sexton said. He looked at his wife. "They didn't try to follow me a while ago, did they?"

Moira shook her head. "Go on, John."

Head bowed, Elwood sat like a lump on the ride down the valley. The Renaults came out with questions. Sexton shook his head and rode on. Nafinger and his boys were working on a distant fence. Sexton told Mrs. Nafinger that the water would be

63

down soon, and said no more.

Donn Lindstrom was repairing his mower. He looked at Elwood's bandaged foot and shouted, "You shoot this man?"

"No. The water will be down soon, Donn."

"Ah!" Lindstrom went running toward the creek.

His wife shook her head. Her face twisted with a worried expression. "This will make trouble, then?"

"If it does, I'll take care of it," Sexton said.

They rode past the bloating sorrel lying in the creek where it had foundered. "See that, Elwood? That's something more to charge to the Stalcups."

Elwood peered dully at the horse. "You think I'll be able to ride again, Sexton?"

"Ask Irv, not me."

Elwood's temper scattered his lethargy. "Wait till he finds out about this. You think you can handle —"

"There won't be any waiting. I figure to tell him myself."

The town was dull with the weight of heat. Sexton swung down in front of McRae's drugstore. He could see the doctor inside, his beard dipped toward a mortar, his right hand using a pestle.

McRae saw the riders; he must have seen the dripping red lump beside Elwood's stirrup. McRae went on with his work.

Sexton saw two men staring from the shade of the livery. The word would be around soon. He wondered if the Stalcups were still in town. "Work that good leg over the saddle, Elwood. I'll carry you."

He took Elwood over his shoulder like a sack of potatoes and carried him into McRae's back room. The doctor barely glanced at the wound before he began preparing a syringe of morphine.

"How are the boys, John?"

"All right, so far."

"Keep an eye on them."

The room was miserably hot. "Are the Stalcups in town, Doc?" Sexton asked.

"They were this morning. They may be here yet." McRae made the injection and began to massage the area around the needle mark. "Don't go away, John," he said when Sexton turned toward the door.

The soporific put Elwood under in a short time. His face was drained and pale, and the sweat lay on it like cold dew.

"What do you think?" Sexton asked. "Can you save that foot?"

"Maybe." McRae rubbed his beard on his shoulder. He counted Elwood's pulse, then put a blanket over the man and motioned Sexton into the front part of the building.

"Yes, the Stalcups are still here, John. Irv is trying to get over a drunk. He's tried to fight everybody in town."

"I'll be glad to accommodate him."

McRae's small eyes pinched down and held Sexton in a narrow grip. "Losing the girl has thrown an awful kink into you."

"That has nothing to do with it! They were stealing water. They left Elwood there to guard their filthy dam. I tried to talk him into —"

"I'm not interested," McRae said. He rummaged under a counter and rose with a sawed-off shotgun. He broke it and it was loaded. He snapped the barrels down again and gave the piece to Sexton. "I had to pry that loose from a dying man before I could even examine him."

He went back to his patient.

Sexton stepped out on the walk. He had thought to go directly to the Stalcups and make his statement. He knew now that it wouldn't work, and maybe it would not have worked even when Irv was not mean drunk.

Kicking through piles of fine dust and breaking cobwebs that gave way with a silky, rustling sound, he crowded between McRae's building and the saddlery next door. He went down a refuse-strewn alley and into the back door of the Sundown saloon. He startled Lew Glinkman, who was standing at the front windows watching men hurrying down the street.

Glinkman stared at the shotgun. His sexless skin seemed to grow more colorless. "Now look, John —"

"I want to thank you for what you did the other day, Lew."

"That's all right." Glinkman kept looking at the shotgun. "Who — what —"

"I had to hurt Stan Elwood. I expect Irv Stalcup to take it up."

"Oh! So that's why he was running just now. Can't you go outside? It's not that I —"

"It's better here." Sexton sat down with his back against the wall. He put the shotgun on the table in front of him. "I'll take that beer now, Lew."

"Sure." That was something which required no thought from Glinkman. He put the glass on the table and stood there, worrying. "Got my sink fixed."

"Fine. How drunk is Irv?"

"Sober now, just feeling like hell. I was awful sorry to hear about the girl, John."

"Thanks, Lew."

"I —" Glinkman peered uneasily at Sexton's expression. The flat brown cheeks were set in hard planes. The mouth was quietly composed, and the eyes were looking at something, or through something, that Glinkman could not understand. He went back to the bar and stood there, fidgeting.

The beer on the table settled into staleness. Sexton thought of something. "Lock the back door, Lew."

"Yes, sir." Glinkman's apron rustled as he hurried past. Sexton heard the bar fall into place on the back door. Then Glinkman stood in the partition doorway, hesitating as if he thought he could not make it back to the bar in time to avoid trouble.

A man ran by on the street, tried to stop before he passed the windows, and could not make it. He appeared an instant later, hands cupped at his face as he looked inside. He ran again.

Glinkman decided the familiarity of the bar was comforting, if not safe. He went there quickly.

"I'm glad you got the sink fixed, Lew."

"Yeah, yeah. It works fine now."

Shadows ran along the front windows.

The Stalcups came in. Five or six men slid in behind them and veered over to the walls. Others crowded the outside edges of the windows, staying on the walk.

Irv, in the lead, came in with a thumping burst. Will followed as if he had a tow rope on him and couldn't help himself. Both men were armed, Will's pistol in a hand-tooled holster, and Irv's merely stuck loosely under his belt in front.

Irv scattered sand as he came across the floor to stop ten feet short of the quiet man at the table. Looking over his brother's shoulder, Will kept his body shielded.

Still lying on the table, the shotgun was cocked now. Irv merely glanced at it.

"God damn you, Sexton," he said. Pale edges showed around the blistered patches of his scabby face. "All the water you claim wasn't worth what you done today."

"I claim it, and I own it, Stalcup. I don't want you to forget it ever again."

"I'll take it whenever I want it."

"Start right here, then," Sexton said.

He learned more of Irv Stalcup in the next few moments than he had ever known before. A deliberate quietness settled on the man's features as he made his estimate of Sexton. The second glance Irv took at the shotgun was no different from the first: He was gauging a chance and seeing that it was not good. But Sexton realized it was not cowardice or a desire to have odds that held Stalcup back. The swaggering and the loudness were backed by all the courage any man could wish for.

It was, rather, as if Irv had discovered a challenge that was worth while and did not wish to take the pleasure from it hastily.

Will Stalcup said: "Well now, Irv, we got to consider he did bring Stan into town. Maybe we all —"

Irv did not hear his brother. "You're declaring yourself, huh, Sexton?"

Sexton felt no need to say anything. There were two of them. The chance was before them; let them take it if they cared to. He had the advantage, and that was good. A calculating wickedness coursed through him. Let this affair be settled now; it would be better than having it hanging fire into the future.

But he saw a logic in Irv Stalcup as brutal as his own. Irv nodded. "All right, you've declared yourself. You're on, farmer." He turned around unhurriedly, shoving his brother out of the way when Will was slow to move. He went to the bar. "Drinks for the house, Lew. Send the farmer over there another beer." He hooked his arm at the men watching through the windows from outside.

"Yes, sir!" Glinkman said, and dropped the first bottle he tried to pick up.

Sexton left two glasses of beer to grow stale on the table. He walked out, past the Stalcups, giving them his back. He went along the street without hurrying or looking back.

McRae was working now. He had a white rag around his head. Sweat was dripping from his beard. Sexton got a full view of what the gravel-sharpened edge of the shovel had done. Elwood should not have been so unreasonably loyal to Irv Stalcup. No, that was not the explanation.

"Do you think he'll be able to use the foot much after —"

"How should I know?" McRae said irritably. "Take your shotgun and go home."

Unused to the weight, Cabot's pinto tired on the way home. Sexton cut away from the valley and stayed on the hills; he did not want to talk to any of his neighbors. From the sage above his own place he saw the boys cutting hay in the north field. The river was normal again. He started to ride to Mary's grave and then realized the futility of that and went on to the house.

Moira did not come out to meet him. She saw the shotgun when he went inside, but she made no comment when he unloaded it and put it away.

"Did you tell Dr. McRae about the boys?"

"Yes, I remembered."

"Will Mr. Elwood be all right?"

"How should I know?" An instant later Sexton regretted his tone. "I'm sorry, Moira." He put his arms around his wife and held her with the intensity of a man seeking refuge in that which is known and loved. "I've been a crazy man the last few days. I'll line out now and get to work, and then maybe I can forget."

Even as he spoke he knew that the bitterness he was trying to shake away was mocking him.

Chapter 4

The hay fell crisply to the chattering knives. Sexton flushed a nest of cottontails and paused lest he chop some of them up. A hawk making its vigilant, contemptuous scrutiny of earth-bound things came down like a rock, but it could not penetrate the heavy growth where the rabbits had fled.

The boys were shocking hay, talking loudly as they worked. The yellow of their wide-brimmed straw hats flashed in the sun. Each day had increased the chance that they would not get the fever; by now they were fairly safe, McRae had said. Strong sons working hard, argumentative, no longer deferring quietly to Sexton's every order.

He knew that all three of his boys had given him less trouble than he alone had given his father. He had reason for pride and he tried to hold it to him; but his gaze strayed to the white fence on the hill and a rankling sensation touched his mind.

The steamy, not unpleasant, odor of the

team came back to him, overswept by the odor of the hay. It was as hot as ever, ideal weather for the work. He saw Moira's washing on the line at the house and the gray tarpaulin rigged on the shady side of the building.

When Moira saw them coming in for supper, she would wet the canvas down. There would be lukewarm water for them to wash the dust and sweat of the fields from their bodies; and then they would eat at the table under the canvas, and rest thereafter, knowing that a good day's labor had been done.

It had been that way before; but Sexton did not look forward to the end of the day now. Part of his life had been ripped away, and the wound would not heal. He spoke to the team and resumed his work. When he came again to a nest of rabbits he did not stop, and one of them, twisting frantically, confused by the team and the clacking knives, leaped the wrong way. It shrieked against death as the mower passed on and left it kicking in the fallen grass.

"Dad! Hey, Dad!" Cabot was yelling, but Sexton did not hear him until he ran up beside the team. "The Belknaps are coming."

"They can see we're busy," Sexton said.

But he stopped a few moments later. He looked at the distant buggy. There was one rider beside it, who would be Helen Belknap, the tomboy of the lot. Even at the distance, Belknap's matched team of blood bays was beautiful.

"Take the mower," Sexton said.

"I thought I'd better go in and get some more water. The jugs are warm and —"

"The creek is closer."

Cabot removed the bandana around his neck. He shook the cloth. "I need another pitchfork, too. Mine is —"

"You figure to use two?" Sexton grinned. "Maybe Helen isn't with them."

Cabot knew the grin. He started toward the house. On the way he had a sudden thought; he detoured to the creek and washed his face and arms.

"Malcolm!" Sexton called, and the youngest boy came on the run, for a chance to drive the mower pleased him well.

"We'll take turns on it!" Roman yelled.

"Do that," Sexton said, "without any fighting." He started toward the house. There was hay to burn, he thought, and someday he might have to do just that to plow the ground where his stacks were. But the thought irritated the deep farmer instinct in him: the growth of the earth was meant to be harvested and used.

Rose Belknap and two of her girls were sitting under the tarpaulin with Moira. Harriet, who had been sick, was still pale. She was the ugly Belknap girl, heavy-boned, dish-faced, with a thick-bridged nose. Martha, who was ten, reflected the fragility of her mother. There was only one word Sexton knew for Rose Belknap: gentle-woman.

Her skin was faintly pink, with the clean softness of Lew Glinkman's face. She was a small woman with tiny hands and feet that were always properly presented. While she was not fluttery, there was an aura of helplessness about her. It was said that she never cooked a meal, a rumor that Moira denied. She and Mrs. Belknap had been friends since the first week the Sextons came to the country.

Sexton made his greetings courteously.

Rose Belknap said, "We've been in Meldrum Park for nearly two weeks. We heard just two days ago about Mary. You and Moira have all our sympathy, John."

"Thank you." Sexton looked at Harriet. "How are you feeling now, young lady?"

"Very well, thank you. As soon as we got out of the heat, I felt fine."

"That's good." Sexton looked toward the

corral. Belknap was unharnessing the blood bays. Helen and Cabot were standing by the rails, arguing about her buckskin.

"Don't think he isn't big enough to last," the girl said. The sun had tangled the colors of her blond hair. Her eyebrows were heavy, her gray eyes clear and wide. After Cabot had been around her he was so dreamy he could not remember his own name.

"He might be all right," Cabot said, "but I can run him into the ground with my pinto."

"Nobody but Indians and kids ride pintos, Cabot. You know that. You ought to come over and get some good horses from my father."

"I'll think about it," Cabot said.

"Where's your father's sorrel? That was a Belknap horse, sired by Red Wing, out of —"

"He foundered the day my sister died."

Rose Belknap said: "Helen talks of nothing but horses. I swear the child would like to be a jockey."

"Child?" Mrs. Sexton smiled. "She's three months and a day younger than Cabot, and he'll be seventeen the fifth of October."

"Isn't that a fact?" Mrs. Belknap sighed, but there was nothing vague in the speculative expression she bent on the young people at the corral.

Sexton drew conclusions that started a small twisting of anger.

"They're going to stay for supper, John," Moira said. She touched Harriet's dress. "Is that some of Joe Allen's material? It goes so well with your eyes." She turned to Mrs. Belknap. "Don't you think so, Rose?"

"We thought it was very pretty," Mrs. Belknap said.

Harriet's eyes were the only attractive feature of her face, Sexton decided. They were clear gray, like Helen's, but sometimes they carried the half bewildered, half resentful expression of one who knows she is less attractive than her sisters.

"I'm glad you're staying," Sexton said. "Excuse me, Rose, girls." He went to the corral to help Belknap.

Frank Belknap was a man of medium size, with a straight back and general bearing like a spring steel blade. Everything about his face was sharply, though not bleakly, outlined, a nose with only slight flaring at the nostrils, small-cusped teeth, white and even, and a jaw line so trim that normal chewing emphasized the muscle-

78

bunching at the hinges. His hair was graying. He kept it cut quite short.

Precise in speech and manner, he shook hands with Sexton and expressed his sympathy. Sexton decided that the man was completely sincere; and then he wondered why he had been questioning every kind word said to him since Mary's death.

"Did you ever see it so hot?" Sexton asked.

"Yes." Belknap nodded. "The year after my father died we had a summer like this. I recall that the following winter was the worst I'd ever seen." Belknap glanced casually at his daughter and Cabot.

Oblivious to the world, they were talking of the next dance at Rock Creek schoolhouse. Cabot was sprawled against the corral rails in an ungainly position.

"Yes, I recall a summer like this," Belknap said.

He was sometimes such a literal, careful-talking man that Sexton wondered how he controlled the twenty-odd men of his crew and his foreman, Tracy Cummerford, who had once been a hard-bitten pistol tough. There was, however, no doubt that Belknap ran his ranch. He hired his own men and fired them personally, and tough young hellions who started at the K either settled down to work or did not last two weeks.

"I'm quite sure it was the summer after my father died, Sexton. You never knew my father, did you?"

"No." It was said that old Scott Belknap had been a hell-for-leather pioneer. Sexton was not sure that the strain had slipped; still, Frank Belknap always puzzled him.

"He was a remarkable man," Belknap said. "He came here in May of 1843, the first trip out, that is. I remember when he returned home. I was only four at the time." He paused. "Have I told you this before?"

"Yes."

"Thank you. I admire frankness." Belknap glanced again at his daughter and Cabot. "What tonnage do you figure on your hay, Sexton?"

"As near as I can tell, it averages close to three tons per acre."

Belknap nodded. "My estimate too. That's outstanding for this part of the country, you realize. The other three farms below here fall short."

"I've a great deal more subwater than they have. I'd still get hay here in any kind of year. By the way, you heard what happened to the creek?"

80

Belknap's nod was a neat little motion. At once he seemed slightly stiffer.

"What do you think about it?" Sexton felt an urge to prod.

"I am not a lawyer."

"I know what the law is," Sexton said. "I'm talking about the principle involved."

"Principle and law should go hand in hand."

Sexton grinned at the evasion. "I understand what should be. I'm merely asking for a personal opinion."

"Why?"

"You're a cowman."

"So I am, but you're implying that there is a conspiracy among cowmen against farmers."

Sexton did not know whether the man was slippery or just exasperatingly logical. He was irritated; he wished he had not brought the subject up.

"It implies a solidarity which does not exist," Belknap said. "To my knowledge, there has never been any ill will between ranchers and farmers in this part of the country. Has there?"

"I guess not."

"My father once ranged cows in this valley, Sexton. He neglected to make any filings, an unfortunate habit of the times

81

which I have not completely overcome myself. A group of people took up this valley practically overnight. Mark Nedderman homesteaded part of what you now own. There never was, as I recall, any trouble between him and his group and my father or any of the ranchers who were then beginning to run cows in the Sawatch."

"All right," Sexton said. "Never mind the opinion."

"I have one, of course, but it is hardly relative unless you feel an urgent need for it."

"I said I give up, Belknap."

Belknap was silent for a time. "This winter I'd like to buy hay of you again. Will the price be the same: three dollars a ton?"

"It will."

"Last winter I used five hundred tons — four hundred and seventy-eight, to be more accurate. This winter I want more, perhaps two thousand tons. I want an option on that much. I will guarantee to buy one thousand tons. So far, is that satisfactory?"

"Fine." It occurred to Sexton that Belknap could have beat the price down by getting bids from the other three hay growers. "Is there any reason you want my hay, in particular?"

"There is. My father always said the grass on these meadows was better than anywhere on the creek. I don't know about that, but I respect his opinion." Belknap paused. "Now — how much do you want on the option for the tonnage above one thousand that I do not expressly contract to buy?"

"Why, hell — nothing."

"There should be a consideration."

"There is: my word that you can have any amount of hay you want up to two thousand tons. Make it four, if you like. I'll have more than that after I finish stacking this year's cutting."

"I respect your word," Belknap said crisply. "But to protect both of us, I prefer to have a legal document drawn."

The anger that had started when Sexton saw Rose Belknap worrying about Cabot and Helen developed a little more. "You can have my word, Belknap. I don't think you'll need two thousand tons anyway."

"Please let me judge my own requirements and methods." It was characteristic of Belknap that he seldom became nettled. "I wish to buy one thousand tons of hay at three dollars a ton, place of delivery, this farm. In addition I wish a second thousand tons available if I need it, at the same price, at the same place. To ensure that the second amount will be held for my use, I am willing to pay a reasonable sum."

"I understand." Saxton watched Cabot twisting his joints as he lounged close to Helen.

"Then I shall have an agreement drawn," Belknap said.

Young people in love, Sexton thought; they did not need written contracts. He remembered when he and Moira had smiled at each other and he had been as nervous with his body as Cabot. And he remembered, too, that he was still in love with Moira. Someday Mary would have met a young man . . .

"To hell with the agreement," Sexton said curtly. "You have my word. Did your father always run to a lawyer every time he made a deal?"

"There were no lawyers here in his time. And there was a difference in the times, also. Today —" Belknap was not one to leave a thought unfinished, but this time he stopped, studying Sexton sharply. "Very well, then. The agreement is made." He put out his hand.

It was another formal sealing that irritated Sexton; but he shook hands.

"Shall we join the ladies?" Belknap said.

"In a minute. There's something that sticks in my mind, Belknap. I needed a horse when I went by your place looking for the doctor. Linneus Carrothers refused to lend me one. It was in my mind to take one anyway." Sexton hesitated.

"Yes."

"Suppose I had done that. How would you have taken it?"

Belknap stared. "That's an odd question, particularly since the event did not occur. You needed the horse badly; you should have taken it."

"Carrothers said no. He was in charge."

"Sometimes Linneus —" For the second time Belknap did not finish a sentence. "Under similar circumstances, if they happen again, by all means take a horse or anything else you need at my place, Sexton."

It should have been a satisfactory answer and Sexton knew it; but he would not stop. "You still didn't answer the question, Belknap."

"I can't. You're dealing with an abstraction. That's not like you, Sexton. Shall we join the ladies?"

"Yeah."

Belknap walked with an awkward horseman's swing to his gait. It was one of the very few things about him that was not neat to the point of pompousness. Going toward the house he said: "Cabot is a handsome lad, Sexton. He favors you a great deal, I would say, although he has his mother's grace."

Cabot, graceful? Sexton twisted around for a quick look at his son. Belknap was not given to flattery; there were times when Sexton felt himself sliding toward a strong liking for the man. He said, "I could use two good saddle horses out of that hay deal."

"That's agreeable. Come over and pick them out any time you wish." A moment later Belknap was bowing to Moira as if he had not greeted her ten minutes before.

They ate from a trestled table under the damp tarpaulin. A sundown breeze rolled the faintly smoky odor of drying hay from the fields. Cabot was most careful of his manners, although he had a tendency to say "Huh?" to any question directed at him by anyone other than Helen.

Roman and Malcolm were having a private little field day, nudging each other and grinning; and then they quieted down when they saw their mother watching them with a calm expression. Harriet Belknap picked at her food. Her eyes kept straying to Roman, who was fifteen. When Roman finally caught on, he finished his supper hastily and excused himself, and presently Malcolm joined him.

Mrs. Belknap talked about the heat, and about the coolness of the Belknaps' summer camp. A camp, Sexton thought; it was better and larger than the house here. Dissatisfaction that he knew was largely of his own making kept churning in his mind. He was particularly aware that Rose Belknap missed nothing that passed between her daughter and Cabot.

Helen and Cabot excused themselves. They wandered toward the creek. Sexton saw how Mrs. Belknap's eyes kept flicking toward them; and then she glanced at her husband. But Belknap was being attentive to something Moira was saying.

Moira had made a quick switch to her best dishes and silver. Sexton noticed that the Belknaps accepted them without comment, although once when Harriet turned a fork idly, examining the lettering on the handle, Mrs. Belknap patted her hand down with a casual gesture, at the same time listening to her husband as he explained what his father had always said were certain signs of a hard winter.

They were only small impressions that

made Sexton think his family was being patronized. Some of them, he knew, he was imagining, but the feeling grew.

Once Belknap said, "Of course, Moira, you get a little more heat down here than we do."

Sexton pried at the statement. The K home ranch was the best in the country. All the girls had separate rooms. There was a dark-paneled office where Belknap kept his accounts. All business matters at the ranch, no matter how trivial, must always be discussed and settled in his office, and afterward there would be a drink and a cigar.

There was a great dining room that looked out on the mountains, and in the summer the upland breeze came gently through the windows. Yes, there was less heat at the K. And if one of the girls sweated a little, the Belknaps could go to their summer home above the shining beaver ponds in Meldrum Park, and stay as long as they wished in a cabin that was better than the Sexton house.

While the women were carrying dishes inside, Sexton and Belknap moved their chairs into the open. Belknap produced a leather case and offered Sexton a cigar. They sat there smoking, Belknap precise even in his relaxation.

"You're really expecting a hard winter?" Sexton asked.

"It could happen. I'm a man of habit, Sexton, and I never forget that some things seem to follow a more or less orderly routine." Belknap carefully licked down the curling edge of the wrapper on his cigar. Satisfied, he asked, "Is there a reasonable market for baled hay shipped from Nelson?"

"No. Between the freight rates and the price I'd have to take in Benton or Cottonwood, I couldn't make the price of a good baler if I shipped all the hay I've got."

"I see. It would be the same, of course, with the others down the valley."

Naturally, Sexton thought.

"If you need help with this year's cutting, I can send you ten men," Belknap said. "Until fall roundup I can spare them."

"Thanks, Belknap. When we get to going in full stride here, we all pitch in together and handle it all right. It's just a matter of good weather then."

"You'll have it."

Belknap's sureness about even the weather was another rake through Sexton's irritation.

He went back to a subject that Belknap

had evaded once. "You probably heard I had some words with Irv Stalcup over the creek. How do you size up Irv?"

Belknap hesitated. "He's a good cowman, in most ways."

"As a man, I mean."

"He keeps his word."

I see, Sexton thought, nettled. Between cowmen a verbal agreement was fine. "How far will he go in a fight?"

"What kind of fight?"

"Any kind."

Once more Belknap licked down the curled edge of tobacco wrapper. "He will go the limit, Sexton." He rose. "I don't like to accept your hospitality and then run, but we do have to be getting home."

Sexton and his wife stood together in the dusk while the buggy rolled away. Cabot and Helen were riding behind it. Cabot would go as far as Little Johnny Hill and then return.

From the barn, where he and Malcolm had been exercising on a trapeze, Roman yelled, "Be sure and stay close to the buggy, Cabot!" He and Malcolm laughed.

Moira sighed. "It was nice to have them here. I like Rose."

"Yeah."

"What's the matter, John?"

"Why is there always something the matter with me?"

Moira put her arms around him. Suddenly she was crying. "I miss her too. Do you think it was easy to sit there tonight and watch Rose and her three girls and not remember?"

"I've been thinking of myself too much." Sexton held his wife tightly. He kissed her with a tenderness that had never been lost between them. Out of their mutual grief and their steadily burning love for each other came the strength that was at once a forgetting and a solace.

It has to be like that, Sexton told himself, *for there is nothing in the impersonal flowing of the world to reach out and touch the problems of individuals.*

He was awake after his younger sons and Moira were asleep. Cabot came in from his escort ride, silent with his own dreams. He went to bed, and the house was still except for the creaking of framing members that were losing the last of the long day's heat.

Sexton decided that he was finally at peace with what had happened. He would bear down in his work again, looking onward once more, forgetting the far ground of the past. And then he remembered that for ten days he had been working like a fiend, and it had not wrung the discontent from him.

He eased out of bed quietly and stood at the window, looking across the shadowy night at the dark hills. A feeling of unrealness came over him; he was apart from everything around him: the woman who slept quietly in the room, his sons in another part of the house, and the land out there that had been the best he ever wanted.

It had been that way in the war sometimes when he went out in front with Berdan's sharpshooters and saw the gray skirmish line bending toward him; and then he had been alone among the men with the smart green uniforms and heavy rifles, wondering whether a brigade or an army was coming up behind the skirmishers.

He was a farmer and the soil was his life, but something had drained the magic from hard work. Tonight he could not see grain fields stretching clear to Renault's line fence; he saw only a lifetime of labor that would never return him the things that Frank Belknap had.

With dark suspicion he wondered how much of the Belknaps' visit had been social and how much business. They had gone home and perhaps Rose had said, "I don't like that boy's mooning around Helen." And Belknap had said: "I bought the hay I needed. He wouldn't have anything to do with a formal agreement."

One trouble bred another as Sexton stared into the night. By now Stan Elwood, whose greatest sin was loyalty, might be crippled for life. Irv Stalcup, who had backed away from the malevolence of a cocked shotgun, and not from Sexton or a fight, was probably making plans.

He keeps his word. He will go to any limit in a fight. Would you care for another of my good cigars, Sexton? We cowmen can afford to treat you hayseeds politely.

Sexton's thoughts veered, seeking an outlet for his racing mind. Irv Stalcup's lips writhed away from his teeth and all the insolent energy of him was in the roll of his shoulders. *I'll take that water whenever I want it. What can that farmer do about it?*

Sexton went into a storeroom at the back of the house. From hooks on the wall he took a dusty rifle. "Let Colonel Berdan's men have breech-loaders, if that is what they want," Abe Lincoln had said. This was one, a Sharps with a cumbersome telescopic sight taken from a sniper's muzzle-loader.

Eyes closed, Sexton held the rifle to his shoulder. He was on a ledge above the falls of Agate Creek, looking down at distant figures wading in the stream. The rifle made its bitter odor and a man, drifting face down in the creek, was no longer interested in stealing water.

"What is it, John? I didn't hear you get up." Moira was in the doorway, a shadowy mystery in a white gown. "What's the matter?" She came close, and there was a pleasant odor from her hair and from the clean warmth of her body fresh from sleep.

"Nothing," Sexton said. "I was just remembering the war, I guess." He put the rifle away.

"That was so long ago. Cabot wasn't born the first time you went away, John. I didn't think the war ever haunted you."

"It doesn't."

"You're not thinking of the Stalcups, are you?"

"I couldn't sleep; that's all it amounts to."

"Did Frank say something that got you all upset?"

"He ordered three thousand dollars' worth of hay, and may want more. Why should I be upset?" Sexton drew his wife to him. His hands were strong and she was

94

beautiful even when he could not see her. Desire that had never been corrupted rose in them. The house was still and sleeping.

"I love you, Moira."

"I love you."

The problems and the worries of the night dissolved. Sexton carried his wife back into the bedroom, and the endless flowing of life that he had considered himself apart from engulfed them both.

But in the gray hours of dawn he was awake again. Coyotes were crying on the hills. Their voices were centuries of lament calling, "Mary is gone, John Sexton, and you are a lonely, discontented man."

They mourned until light began to creep into the room. They stopped as if a signal had been given.

Another day was here. Sexton thought of it with savage dislike.

Chapter 5

Sexton and his sons worked until noon, and all the while a plan was forming in the father's mind. It grew and the work became drudgery and he wondered why he had never questioned his love for the soil. After dinner he told Moira: "I'm going to Nelson on business. Do you want to ride in?"

"In the middle of the day?"

He did not answer or urge her to go. She studied him a few moments and said, "I've too many things to do."

He went to the bridge where his sons were cooling their feet in the creek. "Cabot, you go to the Belknaps' this afternoon. Pick out two good saddle horses. I've made a deal with him."

Roman said, "The hay —"

"Let it rest. By the time we stack what we've laid down, the whole valley will be ready to cut and then we'll have to help Nafinger because it's his turn to be first this year."

Cabot was putting on his shoes. "Two

horses." He grinned. "I'll get the best they got!"

"You'll probably pick a pair of muley cows," Roman said. "Once you get around Helen Belknap you won't know nothing. I'd better go along."

Sexton grinned. "Never mind, Roman. You and Malcolm can go to town with me to pick out the saddles."

Cabot strode toward the corral. Sexton watched him with pride. A big lad, Cabot, and maybe he did have some of the grace Belknap had mentioned. Sexton followed him.

"Now it may be that Belknap will offer you a cigar and a drink of wine. Take the cigar, if you think you're man enough."

"I may take the drink too, if it's whisky."

"Don't get smart. You heard me." Sexton smiled as his oldest son rode away.

Bill Nafinger and his two sons were working on a sulky rake in the shade of the cottonwoods behind their house. Nafinger straightened up. His shirt was soaked, plastered darkly against his broad, thin chest. "Headed for town, John?"

Sexton nodded.

"By God, I'm glad of that. I need some bolts and stuff I didn't figure on. Come up to the house and I'll write it down."

On the way, Sexton asked, "How much hay you going to have in stacks after this cutting?"

"Altogether?"

"Everything."

"Never tried to figure it out, John. I've cut every year because I more or less had to. Last winter I sold three hundred tons to Jim Champe and a dab to the livery. I guess I'll have about three thousand tons this year, altogether. Why?"

"I might want to buy it."

They were at the corner of the barn. Nafinger stopped. "Has the heat got you?"

"I might want to buy it, Bill."

"What the hell for?"

"Speculation, let's say."

Nafinger pulled a splinter from the brown wood. He chewed on it slowly, staring at Sexton.

"I'll give you a hundred dollars for an option on twenty-five hundred tons," Sexton said. "That gives me first right to buy any hay you sell. You get the hundred whether I do or not. I'll give it to you tomorrow."

Nafinger cocked his head. "You're in a stew. What's behind this?"

"I'm gambling."

"You're throwing away a hundred dollars, you mean. What's the price, three dollars?"

Sexton nodded.

"In case you buy, the hundred applies on any hay I sell you?"

"Yes. I'll want an option good till the first of May, next year."

"I see," Nafinger said. "Suppose Champe comes to me again and wants, say, three hundred tons like he did last year. He has to go to you because I'm tied up with you. You try to squeeze him and he won't buy. Then I've thrown away nine hundred dollars for a hundred."

"Have you collected from him yet?"

Nafinger stared at the ground. "Not all of it. He owes me for half of it yet. He's a bastard to do business with, John."

"I know. Let me do business with him, Bill. If he wants any of your hay this year, the first thing he'll do is pay you for what he still owes. Then he'll pay cash for every bit he takes from here, and the same with anyone else."

"All right," Nafinger said. "Bring the paper when you come back from town."

Sam Renault's place was in the narrowing of the valley, less than three hundred acres, with no subwater. Renault had inherited the farm from a cousin, and he had

99

done little with it in the two years he had been there.

Fanny Renault was a large, smooth-faced woman with a sort of bright beauty that played restlessly on her face. She was ten years younger than her husband. The oldest Renault kid was about Malcolm's age. He and his brothers stood around the wagon, a little awed by the Sexton boys.

"Sam," Mrs. Renault cried, "send one of the brats to the creek for that jug of buttermilk. John's kids can have some of that, and I'll make coffee."

The kitchen was already a roasting oven, but Fanny Renault began to build a fire. Sexton studied her husband, taking note of the vague dissatisfaction in the man's expression: Things had not worked out here, but they surely would somewhere else.

Renault pushed a pile of dirty clothes from a chair so that Sexton could sit down.

"You're serious about wanting to sell, Sam?"

"Damn' right, but who's got —"

"I'll give you a thousand. Cash."

Renault opened and closed his mouth. "Hell, I've put that much work into the place since I been here."

"We all do that."

"It's great hayland, John. If a fellow

100

bought a baler and then caught the market just right some year in Cottonwood —"

"You can always catch those mountain freight rates just right," Sexton said. "They raise hay around Cottonwood too, you know. It goes begging at two and a half in the stack. Baled hay —"

"I got some mighty good machinery here. Just a little repairing that I ain't been able to get at and a man would be set to make some money."

"Sure." Renault did not have a decent plow on the place. His mower was beyond repair, but every year he talked of fixing it, and every year he borrowed a mower.

"You really got the cash, John?"

"I'll raise it."

Renault's eyes narrowed. "Just why do you want the place?"

Sexton grinned. "You've been telling me how good it is. It was your idea to sell. If I raise the money I'm as good as any man to buy, ain't I?"

"Sure, sure, but —"

"A thousand in cash, Sam. That includes what hay you have in stacks and this year's cutting, put up."

"A thousand ain't much, considering the work —"

"It'll take you to Oregon in style."

"It would!" Mrs. Renault's face was alight.

Sexton made a cold judgment, comparing her with Moira. He guessed he knew what part of Renault's shiftlessness was due to.

"We'll get out of here and make a decent start," Mrs. Renault said. "That's all we need."

"If I was leaving, I don't much see the sense in putting up the hay for another man," Renault said.

"You'll have help, the same as before. How much hay have you got now?"

"About fifteen hundred tons."

He had, Sexton estimated, about half that amount. "What do you say, Sam?"

"I'll think it over. What have you got up your sleeve, John?"

Sexton shrugged. "You're the one that first mentioned selling."

"We'll do it!" Mrs. Renault said. "When do we get the money?"

"Come to town tomorrow. We'll get the papers fixed up and you'll get the cash."

"All right." Renault acted as if the decision had been his own.

"No use to say anything to my boys," Sexton said. "They'll pester me."

Sexton drove away a half-hour later. The

boys were still complaining about the buttermilk they had been forced to drink out of politeness. Going toward the southern line fence Sexton eyed the ground critically. His own water right would take care of this place, once the ditches were properly laid.

Donn Lindstrom's narrow stretch of bottom land was well cared for. He raised perhaps half as much hay as Nafinger, and although he had put it up in a workmanlike manner, Lindstrom considered hay the least of his income crops. His interest was in hogs, in barley and oats and a small herd of milk cows. He supplied the town of Nelson with pork and butter and cheese, and even shipped considerable cheese to distant towns.

He talked an hour before he finally agreed to give Sexton an option on hay above his own needs. Sexton's boys got in on the conversation. Afterward, Malcolm asked, "What the heck do you want with more hay?"

"Never mind." There was a driving feeling in Sexton now. He was happy, and he could not allow himself to think that he might be laughed at as the biggest fool in the Sawatch country before the winter was over. Back of his happiness, back of his motives, there lay something that he did not care to question.

Dr. McRae saw the wagon. He came to the doorway of the drugstore and inclined his head, indicating, "Come here a minute."

Sexton did not want to break his stride now. He could see McRae later, and Elwood, if he was still there. He waved at the doctor and drove on up the street. At the bank he stopped and got down, giving the lines to Roman.

"Take the wagon to the livery." Sexton flipped a dollar to Malcolm. "Don't spend that all in one place. I'll be busy for an hour or two. When you boys get tired go to the hotel and wait for me."

Malcolm gaped at the dollar. Roman said: "We'll be in the harness shop, looking at saddles. Don't forget."

Joseph J. Allen's general store had a connecting doorway into the bank. Allen owned both places, keeping a clerk in the bank to handle small matters. When Allen was needed in the bank he always removed his apron, a ritual which seemed to change his personality.

This was an occasion when the clerk had to call him. Allen hung his apron on a hook on the store side of the doorway, dusted his hands, and assumed a wary smile. He was a man who weighed two fifty, too large to work, too smart to make a pretense of working. His features were huddled in the middle of his face, an arrangement which made his forehead loom extra large on the outer perimeter of affairs.

He shook hands with Sexton and motioned him into a chair. The clerk resumed work on the store accounts and adjusted his ears.

Allen sat down with a sigh. "Got any warm weather out your way, Sexton?"

"It'll do."

"My wife and I were sorry to hear about the little girl."

"Thanks, Joe."

They got down to business. Allen listened carefully. His features seemed to creep closer together. When Sexton's request was in, Allen said: "You know how hay is. Any one of the four of you out there could supply the whole country. How do you figure to come out on the Renault place?"

"I can do it. All I need is the money until some time this winter."

Allen nodded. "Frank Belknap is buying hay from you again, huh?"

"Some."

Allen sniffed the odor of coal oil on his

hands and his features wrinkled. "Won't Renault take part of the money now?"

Sexton knew the play. He had about five hundred in the bank, and he also had need of it. He shook his head.

"It's a lot of money in times like this." Allen stared as if he had been hurt. "Do you want to cover it with a mortgage on your place?"

"No. Cover it with a mortgage on the Renault place itself."

"Hm-m. That would be included, of course, but the Renault ranch alone —"

"It's worth it."

"My stockholders —"

"You're the stockholders, Allen."

The banker shook his head. "I can't do it, Sexton. If you put your place up —"

"I won't. I hate a mortgage on the ground I have to walk on, or on the food my family eats. I pay cash for anything I buy."

"I know, I know." The pained look stayed with Allen. "If Renault would consider a part payment —"

"He wants the cash."

Allen sighed. "I can't do it."

"Belknap is buying a little more hay than usual this year. He offered to pay me in advance."

Allen nodded. "I know. He's already arranged for part of the money. Yes, I know."

So Belknap had to borrow money too? The thought gave Sexton a feeling of satisfaction. Pompous Frank Belknap, with his eight thousand cows, who talked about his summer camp, and figured his accounts in a paneled office — he had to come here too.

"My word means something, doesn't it?"

"It does, it does. Ordinarily, your word would be good enough — I mean, in average times —"

"The times are average as hell right now, Allen. What do you mean, *Ordinarily my word means something?*"

"I can't do it, Sexton. I'm sorry."

The afternoon had rolled smoothly until it struck this block. The Renault place could be a mistake; maybe Sexton did not need it. But he was playing the plan to the hilt. "I'm sorry too," he said, and rose.

Allen started back to his store. "I've got some beautiful new bolts of calico, Sexton. Did Mrs. Sexton come in with you?"

"No." Sexton was at the front door. Allen's clerk spared him a dry glance.

"John." Allen hesitated. "Irv Stalcup is here. He came in yesterday to take Elwood back to the ranch."

"Does that have anything to do with me not getting the loan?"

"Of course not, of course not!" Allen stepped into the store and began to put on his apron.

Sexton went outside and the sun crashed against him. Anger made his features tight and forbidding. Stalcup was the whole thing. Allen couldn't stand a thousand-dollar mortgage on a farm if the man who was expected to make the farm pay off was dead.

Mort Howell, the station agent, stopped beside Sexton, trying to look as if he had casual business this far from the railroad. He was a deputy appointed by the sheriff in Cottonwood, eighty miles over the Madero Range. He seldom wore a pistol or had any need to. Now he looked keenly for a weapon on Sexton.

"How are you, John? Hot, ain't it?"

"Yeah."

"Sorry to hear about the girl." Howell glanced across the street at the Rangeview saloon. "You heeled?"

"No."

"Got much business in town?"

"Why?"

"Irv Stalcup. He's after trouble. There's no sense in you getting killed."

"That's right, Howell."

"You don't have a pistol, but it still might be a good idea for you to lay low until he leaves."

Disgusted, Sexton merely looked at Howell.

"He'll be leaving pretty soon," the deputy said, half pleading. "All you have to do is —"

Sexton was walking away. He went into the Sundown. There was a small poker game at a table near the arched entrance to the dance hall. Two Stalcup riders were at the bar. Sexton's entrance caused a catch of breath in the card game. Idly, but deliberately, the cowboys swung around to watch him pass.

He went past the men and then came back to them and said, "Anything I can do for you two?"

Their insolence was momentarily jarred, and then they looked at each other and grinned. One of them said, with elaborate politeness: "Not a thing, friend, not a thing. Thank you just the same."

Sexton watched them for a moment longer, angry with himself for letting them get under his hide. "Lew," he said, and went toward the back room.

One of the cowboys said casually, "I

109

wouldn't advise you to give him a shotgun, Glinkman."

Lew Glinkman was nervous from then on. For a time he could bring only half his attention to the words Sexton was saying in the back room. His piece spoken, Sexton said sharply, "Did you hear anything I said, Lew?"

"Sure! Two thousand tons if he takes it all. That's money, John. That's fine." And then Glinkman's own words struck through his nervousness. He sat down slowly.

Sexton said, "If Belknap is right about a hard winter, think of the hay they all will have to have — Belknap, the Stalcups, and Jim Champe."

"Yeah," Glinkman said. "Yeah. But why do you have to buy the Renault place? If you got everything else sewed up —"

"I want that valley under my control."

"A thousand dollars," Glinkman muttered. "That's a lot of whisky piled up in a warehouse, I can tell you. I don't know the first thing about a hay ranch, John. I —"

"You don't have to. You put up the money. You get it back at 10 per cent as soon as Belknap pays me."

Glinkman held Sexton's intense look for a moment and then he looked away.

"You and Joe Allen," Sexton said. "You're both afraid something is going to happen to me."

"Yes." Glinkman's gaze was steady then. "It might happen today, John."

"I'm not worried about today or later. But if you are, I'll insure your money for you. I'll write a letter to Belknap, telling him that the first hay he buys has to come from the Renault place until your thousand and the interest is paid. How's that?"

"Hell." Glinkman got up and paced the room.

Watching him closely, Sexton decided he was trying to rise above his own cautiousness, or fear, or whatever it was.

Finally, the saloonman said: "Never mind the letter. We'll buy the place. You run it. I've always thought it might be nice to have an interest in a piece of ground bigger than a fifty-foot lot in a town that never grows."

"All right," Sexton said evenly. "I'll have Judge Crowley draw the papers and bring them here. I'll send Renault in when I go home in the morning."

Glinkman nodded. All at once he seemed to be wondering how he had got into the deal. When he opened the door and saw the Stalcup riders still at the bar,

111

the worry was all over his face again.

Once more the cowboys faced Sexton, grinning with studied insolence as he walked past them. Again the sun that he always seemed to forget when he was inside ripped into his eyes as he stepped outside. He looked down the street and saw only quietness. At the station, Mort Howell, preparing for the eastbound train, wheeled a truck out to the gravel beside the track. There were a trunk and a saddle on the truck.

Howell was attending to business. He had made token effort to be a lawman, and now the deputy-sheriffing could go to hell. Sexton smiled.

Irv Stalcup smashed through the swinging doors of the Rangeview and stopped under the wooden awning, looking across the street at Sexton.

Any way he's tackled, he'll be hellish rough, Sexton thought. *He's put together like a stud horse and twice as mean.* He waited, giving Irv a chance to do anything he had in mind. The man was still, but the wild energy of him carried strongly across the burning street. Sexton heard men coming to the windows behind him.

It was probably Irv's idea to put on the pressure, to worry Sexton into making the first challenge. After a time, when it was plain that Stalcup did not intend to do anything at the moment, Sexton went on to Judge Hiram Crowley's office.

Crowley was not there. He owned the livery and spent more time around it than he did in his law office. Sexton went on up the street. Irv went back into the Rangeview.

Judge Crowley was lean and bald, with a great hook of a nose. Rusty Nichols said of him that he could hang on a limb by his nose and pick cherries with both hands. Crowley was a tobacco chewer who always spat with a view of hitting something. In Sexton's mind he was as honest as any lawyer could be.

"I've got a touch of business for you, Judge."

Crowley spat at a rock in front of the livery, and hit it neatly. "A little riparian skulduggery?"

"No. That's done, I hope."

"Whatever it is, let's go," Crowley said. "I haven't made a hundred dollars for almost an hour." He started toward his office.

A saddled horse was standing inside the livery, broadside to Sexton. It was difficult to see well, looking from the outside into

113

the lesser light of the building, but he was sure he had caught furtive movement near the horse. "Hold up a second, Judge." Sexton went into the barn. A man's legs were showing under the belly of the horse and the fellow had his head ducked.

Sexton stood still until the man apparently realized the silliness of his position, straightened up, and made a pretense of inspecting something on the rig. It was Jase Purdy, Allen's bank clerk. He nodded at Sexton as he led the horse from the barn.

Like a sheep-killing dog, Sexton thought. He went back to Crowley and they started again toward the judge's office. "Where's Purdy going, Judge? I never knew him to move around on a horse."

Crowley hesitated. "He didn't say."

"You mean it's none of my business."

"It might not be, for all I know," the judge said evenly. "The fact remains that I don't know where he's going." He plopped a shot into the center of a hoofmark in the dust. "You no doubt know that Irv Stalcup is here?"

"Yeah." Sexton watched Jase Purdy riding out of town. The direction was only general so far, but Sexton made his guess. "Have you heard anything about Sam Renault wanting to sell out?"

"No. That's news to me, Sexton."

Then it was news, also, to Joe Allen. Sexton watched Purdy riding briskly through the heat, and he was willing to bet ten bucks against the potato on a coal-oil can that Purdy was hot-footing it straight to Frank Belknap.

Heretofore, Sexton had held business details to be an annoying chore, but now, with the taste of the game in his teeth, he decided he had a grip on something interesting.

They entered Crowley's office. The judge's big nose inhaled stale heat and he said, "Why does a single man stay in this country during a summer like this?"

Forty minutes later Sexton had two option contracts that lacked only signatures. Crowley had the rest of the business straight in his mind. Sexton said: "I'll tell Lew to get you the money right away. You'll see Renault tonight then?"

Crowley aimed at a gaboon in the corner. He missed. "Damn!" he said. "Yes, I'll close the deal tonight. You're sure the rush won't make him want to boost the price?"

"Jingle the money in front of Mrs. Renault if Sam starts to balk."

"You're a trusting soul. With a thousand

dollars in my jeans I could go to Canada. I hear it's cool there." Crowley loosened his string tie. Sweat was gleaming on his bald head. Without changing his tone he asked: "Do you need a good .45, Sexton? I've got one right here."

Sexton shook his head. "I think I'm probably as good with a sixshooter as he is, but I don't want it that way." He looked across the street at the hotel. The boys should be waiting there for him by now. "How *is* Elwood, by the way?"

Crowley hesitated. "Not too good. He's still got the foot, thanks to McRae. I hear he'll never wear a fancy, tight boot again. Couldn't you have used the flat of that damned shovel, Sexton?"

"It's too late to say, Judge. I'll see you at Renault's in the morning." Sexton went out. The street seemed to have gathered tension. A few men were standing under the awning of the Rangeview. Owners of business houses seemed to be concentrating their work near their street windows. The two Stalcup hands were walking toward the drugstore.

Sexton crossed to the hotel. The boys had not been there, the clerk told him. The clerk was nervous. Sexton started away, then turned suddenly. "How much have you got bet, Dale?"

"Five bucks — on Irv." The clerk looked silly, as if he had not intended to tell the truth.

Sexton went back to the Sundown. He told Glinkman about speeding up the deal with Renault, and Glinkman got the unhappy expression of one who has to part with money sooner than he expected to.

"Have you seen my kids go past, Lew?"

"They went to the saddlery."

One of the poker players said, "Cash me in, Mike." The game broke up as Sexton watched.

He went into the bank once more. Allen changed his apron and came through the doorway. He caught the figure on the check as Sexton was writing it. "Yes, sir, fifteen dollars, John."

"Make it silver and put it in one of those little sacks."

"Glad to oblige, glad to oblige."

Sexton hefted the sack, feeling the dollars sliding against each other. "It would be cheaper for Belknap to buy the Renault place than to buy hay, wouldn't it?"

"Now that could just be." Allen appeared to examine the idea thoughtfully. "Of course, it's only in the last few years that Frank has had to buy any winter feed at all. He's increased his herds until —"

"I imagine you could buy the Renault place too, couldn't you, Joe?"

"Why, yes, but I don't understand what —"

"Mind if I get a piece of string in the store?"

"Help yourself, help yourself." Allen forgot to resume his apron as he followed Sexton into the store, and he watched Sexton with a disturbed expression.

Flies caught in strings of sticky-paper overhead were making whining noises with their wings. Sexton glanced up at them once as he cinched his silver dollars in a tight row inside the sack.

Outside, Sexton watched the general converging toward the pharmacy. One of the Stalcup men was holding Stan Elwood's horse down there. The other rider was leaning against the front of the saddlery. As Sexton brushed past him, the man looked at the sky and said, "It could rain."

The unforgettable odor of new leather lay pleasantly in Sexton's nostrils. Roman and Malcolm were fondling two saddles on wooden forms.

"Those rigs won't run off until you get horses under them." Sexton grinned.

The boys began to talk at once. Sexton winked at Emil Siber, the saddle maker. A round-eyed tub of a man, with short, stiff brown hair, Siber smiled briefly; and then he was watching the windows again. After a time Sexton was able to slice a question into the boys' chatter. "What kind of saddle blankets did you settle on?"

"Navajo blankets!" Roman said proudly.

Sexton shook his head. "Couldn't you tell these knotheads anything, Emil?"

The saddle maker waddled forward. "I tried to told dem —" He watched the Stalcup rider leave the front of the building as someone outside gave a curt order. "I vas tolding dem, but —"

"It's all right. They can come back later." Sexton smiled at his sons. "You two scoot up to the hotel and get something to eat. Order me a steak while you're at it. I'll be along in a few minutes." He gambled that they had been so engrossed in their own affairs they did not know what was building up outside.

Malcolm was loath to leave the saddle he had selected. "You won't sell it while we're gone, Mr. Siber?"

"No, no! Now go, like your father said."

Sharply aware of his own tension, Sexton waited until he thought his sons had reached the hotel. In a way it was silly to try to keep them from seeing what was coming. When he had been only a year and a half older than Roman, he had been shooting men with the rifle he had fondled last night.

"Mean, John," Siber said. "Strong like a bull. Very mean. A terrible fighter he is. I haf seen him break —"

"We'll pick the saddles up in the morning, Emil." Sexton put his right hand into his pocket. He walked out.

They were helping Stan Elwood from the pharmacy. His foot was a great shapeless bundle. His tan had faded and his loosely fleshed face was pale. He looked like a man who might be bitter the rest of his life.

Irv Stalcup's gray shirt was sopping sweat from his armpits to his waist. He lifted Elwood into the saddle with an ease that brought a little tightening to Sexton's stomach. The horse tried to sidle, and Irv rapped a curse at the man holding the reins.

The town was here, braving the sun glare, restless with expectancy, looking from Irv to Sexton.

Glancing calmly at Sexton, Stan Elwood tipped his hat down with both hands, shielding his eyes against the bite of the sun, settling himself in the saddle, a man waiting to see a debt collected.

Stalcup said: "You got a good seat there, Stan. You won't miss anything." To the man holding the horse he said: "You let that brute get excited and bump Stan's bad foot against the stirrup and I'll brain you. Depend on that." He removed his pistol belt and tossed it to the other Circle Arrow hand.

Turning to Sexton, Irv said in a matter-of-fact tone, "Do you want to come out here, or shall I haul you off that walk by the back of your neck?" Stalcup's sheer animal vitality was a heavy force.

Sexton stepped down into the street. He heard running feet and from the corner of his eye he saw his sons pounding through the dust to reach the scene. It was just as well; he should have let them stay in the first place.

Chapter 6

Cabot Sexton sat in a leather chair that was stuffed too firmly for luxuriousness and yet soft enough to make him suspicious of its strength. The small taste of wine he had taken was sticky on his lips. He puffed his cigar and eyed history on the dark paneled walls.

There was a Comanche lance that looked as if it still had blood on it. There was a stone maul that —

"I must congratulate you on your judgment," Frank Belknap said. "I would have picked those two geldings myself."

"Thanks, Mr. Belknap." Cabot mixed cigar smoke with the words and some of the smoke tried to back up. He made a great effort to keep from strangling and was successful, but afterward his eyes ran and his mouth tasted like the bottom of a mudflat in late summer.

"Did Helen influence your choice?" Belknap's lips suggested a smile; there was an interested twinkle in his eyes.

"No, sir. She told me afterward I didn't know nothing. She said the bay was a hard-gaited plug and the buckskin a sore-footed stinkaroo that never lasted a full day on roundup."

"Oh?" Belknap looked startled, and then the smile came and lasted a little longer. "She takes after my father, Cabot. He was given to unusual language."

"Yes, sir." Cabot tried the cigar again. He had never seen such an array of arrow-heads, Indian stuff, old firearms, and over the fireplace was a set of polished horns that reached halfway across the wall.

"My father started the collection," Belknap said. "I've kept at it, of course." He rose and shook hands with Cabot as the youth stood up. "Your judgment was sound. I don't believe either of us is worried about Helen's little effort to disparage."

There was a power of friendliness in Belknap that Cabot had never suspected.

"Study the collection if you wish, Cabot. I have some business with my foreman but I'll be back soon. We'd like you to stay for supper."

"Well, maybe I ought to be getting home."

"Think it over." Belknap paused in the

doorway. "The girls helped me find a great many of those arrowheads on the north wall. Harriet is particularly good at it."

Cabot moved slowly along the room. He was excited. He felt good. Old Belknap had treated him like a man. People said that he had no humor and never smiled at anything, but Cabot knew Belknap had warmed up plenty right here a minute ago.

Old Belknap was all right; he might make a pretty good father-in-law.

Cabot studied a rusty cap-and-ball revolver that had been converted from a flintlock. He wanted to take it off the wall for closer examination, but he wouldn't touch it while Belknap was not around to give permission. The dark color on the Comanche lance was not blood, after all; it was rust, Cabot decided.

A soft step sounded in the doorway. Mrs. Belknap said: "Excuse me. I didn't know anyone was here."

"I was just looking. Mr. Belknap said —"

"You should be flattered, Cabot. I've seen my husband wiggle and get nervous if one of the girls even stood close to some of those horrible things."

"They're not horrible."

"That's a man's way of looking at it." Mrs. Belknap came into the room. The

124

movement of her small hands was like a sigh. Her soft, faintly pink face gave her a little-girl appearance.

But the sensitivity of youth revealed something directly purposeful in her eyes to Cabot Sexton. He was at once uneasy before the tiny woman. He felt that he had been trapped in here for a reason. He saw Mrs. Belknap glance at the wineglass. The cigar in his hand was a clumsy, stinking thing and he did not know what to do with it.

He became aware of his rough shoes and his big hands and wrists. With Belknap, those things had not bothered him at all.

"Sit down, Cabot. Perhaps we could have a little chat."

Once more back on the treacherous chair, Cabot's eyes almost crossed as he tried to watch the overlong ash on his cigar and Mrs. Belknap at the same time.

"There's a tray beside you, Cabot."

"Yes, ma'am." The tray was dull bronze, very heavy. Knights in armor rode high-stepping horses around the edge of it. There was not a speck of dust in it, and after Cabot had knocked the ashes from the cigar he was still not sure that he had hit the right utensil.

"That once belonged to a Spanish governor," Mrs. Belknap said. "Do you read much history, Cabot?"

"No."

The woman's hand fluttered toward bookshelves that reached the ceiling in one end of the room. "The girls read all the time, especially Helen. You'd be surprised how much she reads."

There was a Bible in the Sexton home, and out in the barn Roman had a half-dozen Deadeye Dick novels hidden under the hay. Cabot looked at his cigar. He wished Belknap would come back.

"Helen and you do enjoy each other's company, don't you?" Mrs. Belknap laughed indulgently.

"Yes, ma'am, we do."

"She's very much like I was at her age." Mrs. Belknap sighed. "Beaus on either arm, scatterbrained, not a serious thought in my head. Of course, I eventually met Mr. Belknap. That was some years later. Girls must have their little flirtations before they finally settle on a man. Helen is very young yet."

Cabot felt a tightness in his face, a drawing at the back of his neck. He did not know whether he had turned red or white, but he knew how he felt.

"We plan, of course, to send her east to

school before long. There's a splendid school for young ladies near Washington. When the girls were small we visited there one winter. Have you ever been in Washington, Cabot?"

"No."

"Your father has, I've no doubt."

"He marched through there after the war."

"I see." Mrs. Belknap nodded. "I was always under the impression that he was an officer stationed in Washington. So many of Frank's friends were, you know. He went to school in the East. I just guess that I assumed your father . . ." She let it trail away vaguely.

"He was a sergeant in Berdan's sharpshooters," Cabot said.

"Oh? How interesting," Mrs. Belknap murmured. "How I do digress. I was saying that Helen will go off to school one of these days. Such an experience changes a young girl's outlook a great deal. She no longer has — well, shall we say, the same interests that she did before?"

She was sidling up to her point now, Cabot decided. He knew what it would be but he could think of nothing to refute it.

"Two or three years in school," Mrs. Belknap said. "Her outlook will be greatly changed as she learns of something more than this remote little patch of land where we all live. It might be that she won't want to return here." She sighed. "A mother has to face such possibilities. The little ones flutter from the nest. . . ." Mrs. Belknap looked at her hands.

There was a weight in Cabot that sickened him. He was angry, too. He wanted to get up and use his voice loudly, to tell this fragile woman what he thought. He wished he could speak as precisely as Frank Belknap. But he was wise enough to say nothing at all. He began to feel like a lout as Mrs. Belknap raised her head and studied him.

"You're beginning to understand what I mean, aren't you, Cabot?"

"Yeah." Cabot remembered his manners. "Yes."

"I'm very fond of your mother, Cabot. I think you're a splendid boy and I know Mr. Belknap does too." The woman paused. "But what can you offer Helen? In all honesty between you and me, what can you offer her, now or five years from now? Although your father has a fine hay ranch — I know Mr. Belknap has greatly admired what he has done there in the last few years — there are three of you boys. I un-

128

derstand you all work very well together.

"However, you will wish to have some venture of your own someday. I doubt that you will wish to stay with your father and brothers very many more years. What else will you do, Cabot?"

"I don't know." Cabot stared at her. She was as unfair as any grown-up remembering only practical things and nothing else, disregarding everything that lived inside a person. Being young, what was that against anybody? And he could not forget how she had weaseled around to make his father appear inferior to a bunch of political officers who had loafed and gambled and chased women in Washington, while men like Cabot's father were dying in battle.

"When you're older you'll understand what I'm having so much difficulty in saying." Mrs. Belknap smiled.

Cabot's voice trembled when he said, "Do you have to be old to be alive?"

The woman was startled. "I don't quite know what you mean."

"If you were my age, you would." Cabot missed the reaction that made Mrs. Belknap pale. He was looking at the floor; he knew that the feeling inside him could not be transmuted into words.

"I hope I haven't offended you, Cabot."

129

Mrs. Belknap had risen. Her expression said that she had underestimated this boy. But Cabot missed that too.

He stood up. "What you mean is, you don't want me to hang around Helen any more."

"No, no, my dear boy! By no means did I mean that. You're both children. It's all right to be around each other, especially when there are so few nice lads for Helen to know." The steadiness lanced out from Mrs. Belknap's eyes again. "What I mean, Cabot, is not to build up any hopes. That would be causing you later hurt, which I would have you avoid."

She stepped into the doorway. "Well, it was a nice little chat, Cabot. I'm sorry I had to interrupt your study of Mr. Belknap's" — she glanced at the lethal instruments on the walls — "oddities."

The house was quiet. Cabot had no more interest in rifles and artifacts. Still carrying the cigar, he went across the great beamed living room. It was cool. The floor had a mellow, polished glow. He could not help comparing the house with his own home.

He took his hat from a rack near the door. Before he put it on, the fraying edge, the grimy band held his gaze. He knew that small things like that, which he had never noticed before, would stick in his mind now.

"Cabot, I heard what she said."

The lad stiffened. He had not noticed Harriet sitting in a big chair in one corner of the room. The girl's muddy face was set toward him intently. *Why, damn it,* he thought, *she has beautiful eyes!*

"I heard every word," Harriet said softly.

"Thank you." The answer seemed to be quite appropriate, but when Cabot was on the porch, putting on a bold front for anyone who might be watching, he wondered why he had thought the words fitting.

Frank Belknap was coming from the corrals. Tracy Cummerford, his foreman, was riding away. Cabot went down the steps and got the slash of the sun in his eyes. He put the cigar between his teeth.

Belknap said, "Don't tell me you lost interest in my collection so quickly."

"No, sir. I just remembered I have to get back by sundown, Mr. Belknap."

"Oh? You won't have supper with us, then?"

"Thanks. I forgot something at home." Cabot started edging away.

"Some other night, then?"

"Sure. Sure, Mr. Belknap." Cabot went at a fast walk to get the horses. Belknap watched him with a puzzled expression.

Helen was gentling a buckskin colt in the breaking corral. She called something to Cabot. He waved the cigar and grinned, and then he got ready to leave as quickly as he could. He saw the girl watching him, as if offended by his haste, but he rode away without going down to her.

Harriet stood on the porch and said: "You come back again, Cabot. You come back and see my sister."

He waved. He knew then that "Thank you" had been the right answer after all.

Frank Belknap closed the door of his study. "Please sit down, Rosiland."

"Do we have to talk in here?"

"The room has always been satisfactory. What did you say to him?"

Mrs. Belknap raised her brows. "We had a little chat."

"About Helen, I presume?"

"Why — yes."

"What did you say?" Belknap's cigar ashes were spilling on the rug and he did not notice the fact. "What did you say, Rosiland?"

"You know I don't like that name."

There was not even a hint of vagueness in Mrs. Belknap's manner now. "Why, I told him we had plans for Helen, something other than having her marry a destitute hay farmer."

"Did you use those words?"

"Of course not. I pointed out that he was a young man with no definite plans, with nothing to offer Helen."

Belknap shattered his cigar in the bronze tray. It was a deliberate act. His voice, also, was deliberate. "If youth had definite plans worked out, if youth tried to plan its future at the age of seventeen, then youth would be the most Goddamn' dreary era in all mankind's life."

"I don't have to listen to such language."

"You don't mind it a bit, Rosiland. Did you tell Cabot that we were going to send Helen away to school?"

"I did."

"We are not going to send her to school. Harriet, perhaps, if she wishes to go later on. And Martha too, if she is so inclined. But Helen does not need any of your young women's seminaries. Helen has her grandfather's blood. My father, I mean. She belongs right where she is."

"I'm a little tired of your father, Mr. Belknap," the woman said.

Belknap held his breath for an instant. "I will overlook that remark, Rosiland. My father — I will overlook the remark." He walked over to the wall and gazed intently at a flintlock pistol that had been converted to percussion. "Let it be understood that I consider Cabot Sexton a fine young man. He'll do to take along any old time."

"That last expression, Mr. Belknap —"

"That last expression is as honest as he is. My father used it frequently." Belknap turned around. "If, in due time, those two young people, Cabot and our daughter, decide to marry, they will have my unreserved blessing. Every day I find myself considering him more and more like a son, and so —"

"That sticks in your mind, doesn't it? You always wanted a son. You're blaming me because —"

"That's silly, Rosiland. The fact that we have no son is a biological happenchance over which neither of us had any control. I am saying —"

"I know what you're saying. You're blaming me because we have no son." Mrs. Belknap began to weep.

"Oh, hell!"

"Now you're cursing me again!" Mrs. Belknap got more force into her weeping.

"For Christ's sake, Rose!"

Mrs. Belknap flung the door open and rushed away, and her going said that all womankind had been injured.

Belknap went back to his inspection of the pistol. It had been for many years his father's favorite weapon. Belknap was pleased to see that Cabot had not touched it; most men made a grab at it the moment they saw it. He sat down and lit another cigar. The chair was not comfortable. Someday he would go back to those hide-strung thrones his father used to have around. Though he thought about it for a few moments, he knew he never would make the change. Elegance, which he actually did not care about, had trapped him; but since the pretension had never got inside him he guessed the outward showing didn't matter.

Cabot was the problem. Rose didn't know what it meant to strip the manhood from a boy when he was just getting the feel of it, to make him look like a clod, to send him home torn down to the bare, pulsing pride.

Belknap knew what it meant. When he had been fresh from Amherst, fancying himself as quite a blade, having lived down the title of "that wild cowboy," he had courted the daughter of a Massachusetts industrialist. One evening the girl's mother, composed, icily vicious, had made him understand that he was far beyond his depth, that he was, after all, merely the son of a man who raised cattle in some preposterous, uncultured place that was scarcely known to exist.

And perhaps afterward, the woman had called the conversation "a little chat."

Later, the girl wept and agreed with her mother. Since that day Belknap could spot insincere weeping from the first drop. Misty in his memory now, the girl was the least important part of remembrance, but the whole experience was still a fragment that had not leveled away with the settling action of time.

Even without the memory, Belknap doubted that his attitude toward Cabot would be any different.

Harriet came to the door. "Papa, Mr. Purdy is here to see you."

Purdy? Oh, yes, the clerk in Allen's bank. The man did not smoke and he would refuse even a glass of mild wine. Belknap wondered how milk would suit him, and the thought raised faint ticklings of unaccustomed humor. Old Scott Belknap would have growled, *What the hell does that hungry buzzard want?*

Belknap studied his daughter. Rose worried about Harriet, thought perhaps she could never make a good match in marriage. Rose would be happy to settle for some chinless sonofabitch who didn't know one end of a cow from another, if his family connections suited her.

Harriet said, "Mr. Purdy —"

"Would you like to go east to school someday, Harriet?"

The girl shook her head. "They'd make fun of me."

The hurt of truth made little stabs of pain, but Belknap smiled. "You imagine things, Harriet. Tell Mr. Purdy to come right in, will you?"

Belknap listened to his daughter going across the living room. *What the hell did the hungry buzzard want?*

Chapter 7

Irv Stalcup came at Sexton with purposeful deliberateness, not hurrying, not appearing to be acting in anger, but coming in like a man who knew exactly what he intended to do, with no doubts about accomplishing his task.

There was power in his rolling walk, a world of strength in his heavy shoulders. He held both arms raised, with the elbows out, and that left him wide open in the middle. It was the oddest offensive posture Sexton had ever seen; therefore, he was both puzzled and suspicious.

Stalcup's bootheels stabbed little jets of dust. Sexton kept falling back, side-stepping, taking Stalcup in a slow mill. There was a plan in Sexton's mind, and it was a sniper's way: the patience and the long waiting, and then the one sharp blow that was payment.

Stan Elwood sat in his saddle with his mouth half open and his eyes two bitter lines. No matter where this fight had developed, he would have been there, Sexton knew, for Irv would have seen to it.

The thought was an uneasy one, indicating how Stalcup intended to fight, damaging, crippling if he could, paying off for Elwood's foot, as well as for the time he had been turned back in the Sundown.

"Pretty soon, Stan," Stalcup said. "He can't prance around all day."

Sexton tried his left hand then. He speared it into Irv's face with enough snap to make the nerves tingle in his shoulder, hard enough to bend Stalcup's neck a little. The rancher made no attempt to defend himself. He came on again when Sexton stepped back. Once more Sexton cracked him in the face with his left fist. The blow left a purplish splotch on the scabby red skin of Stalcup's cheekbone.

There had been power in it, Sexton knew, enough to have made an average man wary.

"Hell," Irv said contemptuously.

Respect that verged on fear touched Sexton. The man was a physical brute. Meet him head-on and he would daze you with pure force. Long-range hammering would not wear him down, not in this heat. Moving faster all the time than Irv, Sexton was already feeling the effects of the sun.

The sniper plan was best. If that failed, then he was in for a mangling. Stalcup feinted a rush. Sexton backed up quickly, bumping against one of the spectators.

The man shoved him ahead violently. "We want a fight, not a footrace."

Irv could have rushed him then, for Sexton was off balance. Sexton tightened his guard instinctively. Irv chopped his arms down with clubbing blows that were like the bruising from bludgeons of green piñon. Then Stalcup cuffed him with an open hand, a jar that knocked Sexton a full step sidewise before he recovered.

Dropping his arms for an instant, Irv looked up at Elwood. "I'll start pretty soon, Stan. I won't keep you sitting there too long, boy."

It was fear that touched Sexton. Irv might be a swaggerer but he was no empty braggart. He was completely sure of himself. Sexton wanted to cut loose with his payment shot, but he waited. He took another clubbing on the arms and a flurry of casual blows that made his head ring. He saw the contempt in Stalcup's eyes, and the man's dedication to his task.

The chance came from Stalcup's own sureness. He brushed sweat from his face with his left hand and let the hand come down carelessly.

Sexton hit him with his right hand. His big fist was aching tight around fifteen silver dollars tied firmly in a sack, fifteen cartwheels side by side, a solid row of lethal weight.

The blow took Irv fairly on the chin. Even without the extra weight, it was the hardest swing Sexton had ever delivered. He knew it. Stalcup's boots came up as if he had been struck across the heels with a fence post. His arms were still in front of him as his body went back. During the falling distance of his figure, he was in the air for an instant. He crashed on his back under the belly of the horse.

Sexton thought he might have killed him. Irv did not move, and then Sexton was afraid he had killed him.

The onlookers were as quiet as the figure shocked into stillness under the horse. The animal sidled nervously. The holder bore down on the reins and cursed automatically, all the time staring at Irv Stalcup.

"I'll be — I'll be —" someone muttered, and could not find the word to describe his astonishment.

Sexton thought the bones of his hand were smashed. He could barely move his fingers to release the sack when he dropped it into his pocket. Unconsciously massaging the hand, he stared at Irv, and he felt as he had felt after he ruined Stan Elwood's foot.

Then Irv sat up. He rolled at the hips, with his head swaying. Blood was squeezing from the chipped red skin where Sexton's first two blows had landed, but there was no mark at all upon his chin. His eyes were foggy and there seemed to be no intelligence in him.

"You'd better finish him, Dad!" Roman said excitedly.

Sexton kept rubbing his hand. He knew Irv could not rise. The man was done; he had gone down as if he was dead in the air and he had lain helpless for several moments. It was impossible for him to rise.

Irv's gaze fixed on Sexton. The rancher pawed his hand through the air with a waving, groping motion. He found Elwood's stirrup. He hauled on it, and then with a sudden explosion of energy he was on his feet again, rolling in toward Sexton, and now he was coming to kill.

"I won't be long, Stan," he mumbled. "You stay right there on that horse and watch."

Sexton was deathly afraid of the man himself now, but he had never been afraid of a fight itself. You won or lost a fight, and in the doing you dropped all fear of the adversary. He forgot the dollars in his pocket.

He met Irv Stalcup head-on and nothing but force was left.

Stalcup beat Sexton's guard down again, chopping with the bones of his fists and arms and wrists. He hammered Sexton into the dust and walked across his body, stumbling on as if he had an opponent still ahead of him.

One of the spectators, looking straight into Irv's eyes, cried, "Hey!" and fell back to the sidewalk.

Stalcup swung around as Sexton scrambled to his feet. "Oh!" Irv said, and came on again. Sexton beat him in the stomach. He tried to knock Stalcup back with his shoulder and get him clear for another looping swing.

Grunting deep in his chest, Irv beat Sexton to his knees and tried to kick him in the face.

Sexton's battered arms took another jolt before he crabbed away and got on his feet.

"Get up," Irv said. His eyes were still foggy.

It came to Sexton then that the man had

lost track of what he was doing. The deep wells of animal strength were carrying him on, but he would never remember what had happened after the one time he was knocked down.

Survival instinct was carrying Sexton too, dipping into forgotten reserves after his mind told him his arms were too heavy to raise and swing. End it one way or another as soon as possible, he told himself.

This time he went to Stalcup.

Irv was power that kept bulging out like the pressure of a breaking dam. He grunted and blew blood from his lips and there was no end to his will to destroy. Sexton knocked him down once more, and his only feeling was mild surprise that he had been able to do so.

Then Irv was up again and rolling toward him.

Sexton missed the passage of time. He missed all details of what he did. The heat was killing him. A face whose life seemed to be oozing out of purple blotches disputed the thought of dropping full length in the dust to rest forever. Pain came dimly through the red fog that was growing denser. The odor of Stalcup's sweat was a stink to offend him.

He was staggering toward nothing suddenly. He heard a man say, "I won't believe it!"

Irv was down once more, the great bulk of him trying to stir, his fighting will trying to jab life into flesh that felt the signal but could not answer.

McRae's voice was a disgusted rumble. "That's all, boys. Go back to your caves for the rest of the day."

Sexton turned uncertainly. His vision was unclear. He was afraid of his legs, afraid of the poisons that were trying to bring him down. He stumbled into a horse. Someone cursed him. And then a strong arm hooked into his and Emil Siber said, "Inside mit you."

"The walk. Step high, Dad." Roman had his other arm.

Without support Sexton would have fallen over the walk, but he got on it and said, "Wait." He turned his head painfully. Four men, red-faced with heat and exertion, were staggering toward the pharmacy with Irv Stalcup.

Sexton was content then to go into the saddlery, where the odors and the gloom made a contrast that barely stirred in his consciousness. With help he dragged himself into the back of the building and fell on Siber's cot.

At dusk he was sitting in Siber's kitchen, drinking coffee and wondering how the German got it so strong, when he heard McRae enter the shop and start joking with the boys about their saddles. Siber said: "John is fine, Doctor. I put some medicine on him."

"If it works on a horse, it'll work on him." McRae came into the kitchen and helped himself to coffee. Glancing at Sexton's discolored face with sharp professional interest, he sat down and stretched his legs.

"What about Elwood, Doc?"

The doctor gave Sexton a faintly bitter look, and then he was not even thinking of him. "At one time I planned to have a children's hospital back in my home town. That was long ago." McRae tapped the checkered tablecloth with his fingers. "Elwood's foot? He'll walk again, in time. Did you expect it to be as sound as before you tried to chop it off with a rusty shovel?"

"You're in a fine mood."

"Yep!" McRae drank coffee, watching Sexton over the rim of the cup.

"You're still not considering any of the reasons for the trouble."

"Reasons vary, depending on the source. None of them interest me greatly."

146

"You gave me a shotgun the other day, Doc."

"You know what I was thinking of? Mary. I had a lot of feeling for you because of her, Sexton. It twisted my judgment." McRae wiped the back of his hand across his mouth, studying Sexton with clinical detachment. "I think you're getting a little twisted too."

"I couldn't duck that fight."

"I guess not." McRae appeared to forget the whole premise of a disturbing thought. "What did you have in your hand, by the way?"

"Silver dollars. Fifteen of them."

McRae grunted as if he had been hit with the weight. "No wonder Irv has a concussion."

"How bad is it?"

"Oh, he rode home an hour ago. Next week he'll know he had a concussion, but I don't think it'll bother him too much at that." McRae nodded his head. "You picked a real prime bull to try to take to market, didn't you?"

"He picked me."

"All right. He picked you. Let me see your right hand."

The skin was off the knuckles and the hand was swollen. McRae examined it carefully. "Soak it in hot water, and then put it around the handle of a pitchfork and use it. The human body is put together with God's own ingenuity, but of course, by working hard, we can always find ways to destroy it."

He dropped the hand. It whacked the table edge and Sexton winced. "You sure are in a hell of a mood, Doc."

McRae stood up. "How's Moira taking your high didoes?"

"All right," Sexton said evenly. "I don't think she'll make as much fuss as you over a simple fist fight."

"It was none of my business. I admit it." McRae stopped in the doorway. "You can't lick Irv again with your bare hands. You know that, don't you?"

"Maybe."

"Get your shotgun somewhere else the next time you need one. You've asked for more trouble than is needed to patch hell a mile. You went to the right place, too."

McRae went back into the shop, and Sexton listened to him talking to Malcolm and Roman. It was remarkable how different the doctor's tone was then.

At daylight the boys bounced out of bed in the hotel and began to wrestle on the

148

floor. Sexton eyed them sourly. He rose in sections, feeling as if he had fallen from a cliff the day before. *I'm only thirty-five,* he thought; *I shouldn't feel so knocked-out and old.*

He was better after breakfast.

The boys were in a hurry. "All right, all right!" Sexton said, before he had finished his coffee. "Take the wagon down to the saddle shop and wait for me."

A swamper was changing sand in the Sundown. It was an unearthly hour for Glinkman to be up, but he was standing in front of his saloon. "I didn't sleep much last night, John. I'm a little worried."

"You're damned good and worried, Lew. Your money?"

"No, no. That'll come back, I know." Glinkman's long face was lugubrious, but still there was a patient dignity in his manner. "I'm a partner in the Renault place, and I've been thinking about what you've got in mind. If —"

"You don't have to be a partner, Lew. I'll buy —"

"I know you can buy me out when Belknap pays you, but it'll still be me that put up the money. You figure to ruin the Stalcups if things work out right, don't you?"

"I do. And Jim Champe too."

149

Glinkman looked intently at Sexton. "Oh, I see. Christ, John! You still ain't blaming Champe because Doc McRae was out there that day?"

Sexton had not intended to speak Champe's name; it had come from him unconsciously. He kept thinking of the man whose needless act had taken the doctor out of town the night before Mary died. He stared at Glinkman, angered because Glinkman had seen so clearly into his mind.

"Jim Champe too," Sexton said.

Glinkman swallowed. "Belknap?"

"No." Sexton hesitated. "No, I guess not."

"I'm sorry I got into it." Glinkman walked into the saloon.

A rabbit, Sexton thought. He started down the street. A scared rabbit. But he could not hold anger or even contempt where Glinkman was involved. Lew Glinkman was the man who had left his work to ride to the Five Bar after the doctor. There was nothing he could do now to shake off Sexton's friendship.

Joe Allen was sorting potatoes. He brushed his hands and gave Sexton a wary smile. "You're looking good, John, considering."

"I feel fine." Sexton was sore and stiff and he knew that by night he would be worse. "What did Belknap have to say about the Renault place?"

Allen's crowded features pinched in as if they were whispering to each other. "I don't follow you."

"You sent Purdy to see him yesterday, didn't you?"

"Why, yes, on some routine business."

The man was lying, but there was no point in pressing the subject. Sexton hoped that Judge Crowley hadn't run into any snags in the deal with Renault. Sexton said, "I want three pistols and everything to go with them."

Allen was shocked but the merchant in him quickly recovered. "Yes, sir!" he said. When that transaction was completed, Sexton closed his account at the bank. "I'm sure you know what you're doing, John, but —"

"Since you're sure I know what I'm doing, let's not talk about it. Just give me the money." Ready to leave, Sexton said, "Purdy must have had a lot of routine business with Belknap."

"He stayed there all night, I imagine."

"You *must* be imagining, Allen. The hotel clerk mentioned this morning that he

151

came in last night and went somewhere again. Out to Renault's?"

"Maybe. You're an insulting bastard, John."

Sexton laughed and went out. There had been sly triumph in Allen's expression, but the man was in for a shock. He probably did not know that Crowley was ahead of Purdy, and only three men knew that Crowley was carrying cash taken from Lew Glinkman's safe.

The boys were goggle-eyed over the pistols and the holsters. "That second one is for Cabot," Sexton told Malcolm. "You're too young yet."

When Sexton came out from paying Siber, he saw that the boys had strapped the pistols on. Roman tried to take attention away from the fact by asking quickly, "Did you get the bolts and stuff for Nafinger?"

Sexton went through an uneasy moment of wonder. He was not one to forget an errand for a neighbor, but this time he had forgotten completely. He gave the list to the boys. They swaggered up the street wearing the pistols. He started to call them back and then said nothing.

Mort Howell was watching from the station. Before the winter was over, Sexton thought, he might know just how heavy the deputy was. Belknap had a good opinion of the man.

Where West Forsythe came into Agate the Sextons met Jase Purdy, a weary man bumping along slowly, plainly showing his dislike of the saddle. The sourness of his expression convinced Sexton that Purdy had made his trips last night for nothing. Sexton spoke pleasantly and waved. Purdy nodded curtly and rode on.

A few moments later Roman asked, "What are you laughing about, Dad?"

They drove on to Lindstrom's. The Swede had been puzzling over the hay option. Sexton told him the truth again, but Lindstrom spent an hour hesitating before he signed. He blinked with suspicion at the money Sexton put on the kitchen table. It had come too easy.

At the Renault place Judge Hiram Crowley was sitting on Renault's worthless mower. He looked so downcast that Sexton had a quick twinge of fear and asked a sharp question. Crowley worked his cud slowly.

"You and Lew got the place, all right." Crowley hit a rusty tin can at fifteen feet and was still unhappy. "Purdy was here too late, wanting to buy it for Joe Allen."

"Oh!" Sexton realized that he had made a slight misjudgment. Allen had not been giving any free information to Belknap when he sent Purdy to the K. Allen no doubt had been after a hay contract himself, and probably a price cut had been offered.

That Purdy had come here afterward indicated that Allen thought the Renault farm a good buy, whether or not Belknap had been interested in a hay deal. Sexton was pleased with his own minor success. This business was really cutthroat. He began to laugh.

"I don't find a damn' thing funny this morning." Crowley rolled his shoulders and then there followed an involuntary shuddering motion. "I got bed-bugged in that miserable house last night. My fee will be considerably higher because of it. I should have slept in the barn."

Sexton wasted as little time as possible with the Renaults. He drove on up the valley. Bill Nafinger signed the option and took his hundred dollars almost absently. He appeared more interested in the box of bolts and parts Sexton delivered to him.

"I'll be cutting day after tomorrow, John."

Sexton flexed his swollen hand. "We'll be here."

On a creamy buckskin, Cabot charged down to the line fence to meet the wagon. Sexton eyed the horse keenly and decided that it would do. His plans were enlarging with his ambitions. He wondered why he had stopped at two good saddle mounts.

There was an excited babble over the saddles and the pistols. Malcolm was unhappy because he had a saddle but no horse. "You can have Cabot's little pinto," Sexton said. "Some evening Cabot can go back to Belknap's and get another horse."

"No," Cabot said. "It would be better if you went." All his enthusiasm had died in an instant.

"Did Belknap give you any guff?"

Cabot shook his head. "I just don't want to go back there for a horse — or anything else."

Malcolm grinned. "He had a fight with his —"

Sexton rapped his youngest son with his elbow. He watched the sullen, miserable expression on Cabot's face and was worried. Puppy love? By God, no. Cabot was much like his father, and Sexton had been married when he was only a few months older than Cabot.

Moira saw the pistols first of all. She studied her husband's battered face and said, most quietly, "John, I won't have my sons wearing those weapons."

"Now, don't worry about it, Moira."

"I don't want them wearing those guns."

Sexton got down from the seat. "When I was Cabot's age, I was in a war. Before that, not any older than Malcolm, I had learned to use a pistol and a rifle."

Moira shook her head. "I don't care. Those guns do not belong here."

"They stay! You'll have to learn to live with them." Sexton began to unharness. "I bought the Renault place." He told her briefly about his options and about his trouble with Irv Stalcup.

"So then you bought weapons for your sons."

"Yes, I did!"

"Where does it lead?" Moira asked.

"Wherever it will! I'm sick of being a farmer," Sexton said savagely. "I'm taking my chance on something bigger, a chance to leave my sons something more than a patch of ground that won't make them a living."

"You're not thinking of them at all." Moira's face was white. "When you try to turn away from the soil, you're trying to turn away from yourself."

"Soil, hell! Work and nothing, with the

156

Belknaps looking down their noses at me!"

"That isn't so, John."

"Don't tell me!"

"It won't matter if you make a fortune on a wild gamble. You'll be lost."

"I'll risk the chance."

"And drag your sons into it, too."

"They're old enough to start learning that you've got to be hard, to cheat a little, to fight like a fiend for anything you get out of this life."

"You've gone crazy, John Sexton! You're after a terrible fight, you are. You want to destroy the Stalcups and make gun fighters of your own boys!" Moira's tongue slipped toward a brogue that was ordinarily only softly evident.

"You're damned right! I'm after the Stalcups, but that's only part of it."

White of face, her eyes a blazing green, Moira cried, "You know what ails you?" She pointed toward the white fence on the hill. "You'd like to destroy the whole world because of that!"

"Don't say that, Moira." Sexton's voice was trembling.

"It's the truth and I will say it! The day that Mary died —"

Sexton stepped forward and cracked his wife in the face with the back of his hand.

Her head jerked back. A red streak lay across the whiteness of her cheek. She touched the corner of her mouth with her fingers and when she lowered her hand slowly there was blood upon it.

"Now will you be quiet!" Sexton said.

She shook her head slowly, looking at her husband with an expression of pity that infuriated him more than her anger. He raised his hand again. She stared at him so quietly that he knew force was no weapon at all.

"Consider what you're doing, John."

"I know what I'm doing!"

"Do you now?"

"Don't cross-examine me!"

"Then I will not. But I will fight you for my sons, John Sexton. I will fight you to the death."

She waited on him then, leaving the answer to him, so that he could have spoken the regret that nagged him, or have admitted the truth she had hurled at him in anger. Doubts about what he was doing tried to creep in, but a black stubbornness rose up to override all other emotions.

He dropped his hand. "Leave me alone, Moira. Don't interfere."

Her quiet going, the set of her long back as she turned away almost tore a protest from him. Then she had gone into the house and he was standing there tight inside. He looked around for the boys. They were nowhere in sight and he did not hear them. He went back to unharnessing. His hands trembled as he buckled a strap he had unbuckled a few moments before. He stared at it vaguely.

The team jumped when a shot sounded. He knew without looking: the boys were at the creek with the pistols. Later, putting the team away, he looked through the manure window and saw Cabot aiming at a board stuck in the sod on the far bank of the stream. The shots came slowly, evenly spaced, while Sexton was taking care of the horses.

He went outside and looked south toward the Nafinger place. It struck him that he could not recall driving past his oats this morning. Moira came from the house with an armful of bedding. She shook each piece vigorously before she hung it on the clothesline. She gave her husband no attention, going about her work as if there had never been a quarrel.

Sexton hesitated, watching her. And then, after a time, he went around the barn and strode toward the creek to teach his sons how to handle pistols.

Chapter 8

Now the smashing heat had lifted from the land and the days had a golden tone. Each morning frost made a silvery glint on the stubble of the hay fields, dying quickly when the sun rose. Light snows had dusted the Sawatch Mountains. To the west, the higher and more forbidding Maderos showed white patches that would be there until late the following summer.

John Sexton was building fences around his haystacks as if the devil were driving him. Cabot grew tired of the work. He said: "I don't see any sense in this. We've got good fences all around the place, so why should every damned little haystack have —"

"Never mind what you think," Sexton said. "Keep digging."

"There's no sense in it. We don't need —"

"You heard what I said!"

From deep-set eyes Cabot threw an appraising study on his father. There was no insolence; there was, instead, a quietness so much like Moira's expression that it angered Sexton.

"What's the matter with you lately, Dad?" Cabot asked. "Ever since —"

"Never mind your ever-sinces! I said to get to work." All of his sons had stopped working. Sexton glared at them.

"There's no sense in all these fences," Cabot insisted.

"Will you stop your damned arguing! When I was your age and sassed my father —"

"When you were my age," Cabot said, "you'd been gone from home for two years because you couldn't get along with your old man. All I'm trying to find out is what's the use of fencing every stack on the whole place."

His son was right and Sexton knew it, but the black stubbornness was bearing down again. He said, "I'm telling you for the last time to get to work."

"Tell me why," Cabot said, "and then if there's any sense in it, I'll do what you say."

"You'll do it anyway!"

Cabot drove his bar into the hole he had been digging. He started toward the house. Malcolm and Roman kept looking from him to their father.

"Cabot!" Sexton said, "if you keep walking, see that you wind up clear off the place. I mean it!"

The youth did not break his stride and he did not answer. Even in his anger, Sexton thought: *He's more of a man than a boy. He's like me when I was his age.* To lose him now would be the repeating of a mistake that Sexton himself had made. He started to go after his son and then he stopped.

Moira was the answer. She would calm Cabot down and make him understand; she could always do that with any of the boys. And then when Sexton went to the house for dinner, he would meet Cabot on a man-to-man basis and explain his reasons for the fences.

A short time later, working furiously, Sexton saw his sons staring toward the house. Cabot was riding away. There was a pack behind his saddle. Sexton shot a quick look at Malcolm. "I suppose you're going to cry."

"No, he ain't," Roman said. "You're not going to cry, are you, Malcolm?" The two boys took strength from each other. Sexton received the impression that they had joined against him. When they resumed their work he knew that some understanding had passed between them that excluded him.

After a few minutes he went to the house. Moira was mending clothing. That she could go so calmly about routine work both irritated Sexton and roused his suspicions.

"Where did he go, Moira?"

"To see Frank Belknap about a job." Moira clipped the frayed gray edge from a hole in a pair of jeans. Her expression was contained and distant. "I suggested that he try there."

"So that's the way you're fighting me?"

"You made the quarrel, John."

"I depended on you to talk him out of it. I need him."

"Do you need him, or his pistol? He's better off away from here."

"By God!" Sexton said. His wife's steady gaze stopped him. He thought he saw compassion under her cold expression, and that was more to be feared than her anger. He pointed at the pile of mending on the chair. "Look at that! All you have is work, but when I try to do something to get us all away from drudgery, you stand against me. By trying to do the things for you that Belknap does for his wife —"

"Rose is still an unhappy woman. I haven't been, until lately." Moira put her work aside and came to Sexton. She was no longer cold, but the shards of pity were in her expression. "You're wrecking yourself, John, because of something only God could have changed."

"There you go again! I'll be damned if I take your pity. I know what I'm doing." Sexton walked out into the yard.

Cabot had swung along the south line fence and was cutting back toward the hills. Sexton watched him ride to the white fence and dismount. For a very short time Cabot stood there, and then he rode away.

His visit at Mary's grave put a grim clincher on his decision to leave home; before that Sexton had not fully accepted the thought that Cabot was going. The creamy buckskin grew smaller on the hills. Sexton walked back to the doorway of the living room. Still mending clothes, Moira did not look at him.

He went back to his work at a fast walk; he knew what he was doing.

Two weeks later the air carried the chill from snowfields that were creeping lower on the mountain. Indian summer was gone.

Cabot Sexton was punching cows, liter-

164

ally, with a prod pole up an improvised chute into cars at Nelson. The permanent loading corrals were busy too; Frank Belknap was shipping in a hurry.

Rusty Nichols, a grinning gargoyle of a man, was on the other side of the chute. He had argued beyond necessity with Tracy Cummerford, Belknap's foreman, so now he had been unhorsed. Rusty did not seem to care. Neither did Cabot, for he had held the low end of every operation since he went to work at the K.

The riders crowding cows toward the flimsy outwings that fed the chute had trouble with an old ridge-runner steer that looked like a survivor from Spanish times. The steer did not care about the chute or any part of the forcing bustle.

It smashed through the outwing and charged Cabot. He dived under the cattle car, banging one knee on a rail, cursing savagely. The press of riders prevented the steer's escape. Head high, it went back through the broken boards and smashed its way toward Rusty, and he dived under the car also.

Cummerford was watching. A trim man with coarse Indian-brown hair, wide cheekbones, and narrow eyes that gave him an Oriental cast, he had come out of the Na-

165

tions years before, serving for a year as marshal of Nelson when the town had been end-of-the-rails and a hell's broth of a place. For a long time he had been Belknap's foreman.

He watched a rider almost lift his horse away from the rake of the rampaging mossyhorn. Cummerford shot his red roan out and took the steer from the side. He forced it into the broken outwings, and when it would have turned he leaned out from the saddle and whacked it across the face with his quirt.

For an instant it seemed that both rider and steer were trying to go up the ramp. Cummerford stopped, his horse almost going on its rump. Started up the ramp, the steer pawed at the cleats, bellowing. Cabot limped in from one side and Rusty went to work on the other side. Together they poled away until the steer made a frenzied rush into the car.

"Wire the outwings up. Keep 'em moving," Cummerford said. "This ain't no box social."

"I'm glad you told me." Cabot began to wire broken planks together.

Rusty spat dust and grinned. "I remember that steer from away-back. He was eighty years old when I first went to work

166

for Belknap, ten years ago. I think he's just a year younger than Tracy."

Cummerford's glance was humorless. "Less talk, more action."

Belknap had cleaned his range, sending his crew into canyons and thickets where ordinarily he was content to leave a few canny hideouts to grow older. He was holding back a few hundred three-year-old steers and about fifteen hundred cows which had been carefully selected. He was shipping the old and the young and the weak, and some of the stuff would hardly pay the freight.

Cabot knew all the talk, even if his job as cook's helper had kept him close to a roundup wagon.

The cars ran out in the middle of the afternoon. Belknap came back from his fourth trip to the station and surveyed the scene with an exasperated expression. He still had a trainload of cattle on the flats west of town and more to come.

"I bet them telegraph wires are smoking," Rusty said, "but hell, anybody knows the railroad spots cars over here when they get good and ready, not because anybody orders them."

They got help from some of the riders and lifted the chute clear. A brakeman closed the door on the packed mass of cows, and a pusher engine came drifting down from the station to help the fifteen cars over the Maderos.

"Let's you and me get a drink, Cabot," Rusty said.

Cummerford seemed to overhear everything. "A half-hour in town, you two, and then back to the bed ground. Sober, too."

"Like a judge," Rusty said.

He and Cabot tied up in front of the Sundown. The rail was crowded with horses, and so was the rack across the street at the Rangeview. Both Champe and the Stalcups had finished shipping two days before. Inside the Sundown the bar was lined with cowboys in a fine state of after-roundup hilarity.

Cabot heard Irv Stalcup laugh, and then located him seated in a poker game with cattle buyers and a few businessmen at the big table near the entrance to the dance hall. Irv's hat was on the back of his head, he had a cigar in his mouth, a bottle of whisky on a chair beside him — he seemed to be enjoying himself.

In the middle of his laughter he saw Cabot and gave him a sharp after-glance. Rusty and Cabot pushed into the bar. Cabot's pistol jammed against the thigh of a Five Bar rider, who moved over to make room, at the same time glancing down at the pistol, and then casually at Cabot's face.

Somewhere down the bar Jim Champe's voice carried through the gabble. "Sure, he's betting on a hard winter. . . . Belknap backs a lot of odd horses. . . . I remember when . . ."

"We got to work fast," Rusty said. "When Cummerford says a half-hour he means it. Drink up, but stop somewhere short of the falling-out-of-the-saddle stage."

"One will do me," Cabot said.

Rusty grinned. "In that case, you'd just as well stayed there to help haze the leftovers back to the herd." He took his third drink.

Champe's voice came again, "If I need hay, there's plowmen that'll beg me to buy it."

One of Champe's own men murmured to his companion next to Cabot, "Getting their pay for what he buys will be another matter."

Cabot leaned back to look along the row of men at Champe. The Five Bar owner was a half a head taller than anyone in the line. He was dressed no better than any of his riders, a big-nosed man with a large frog-like mouth and tiny eyes that were either glinting with amusement or wickedly bright, depending on whether he was seeking a bargain or being asked to uphold his end of one already made.

It was said that Jim Champe was constitutionally opposed to paying a debt.

Cabot looked down the bar at him and thought: *If he hadn't been so crooked, Mary might be alive today.* He held the thought a moment, saw the futility of it, and forgot it.

"Better have another drink," Rusty said. He was on his fifth. "By the way, have you got any money?"

Cabot shook his head.

Rusty sighed. "I guess I'll have to pay, then."

A few moments later someone tapped Cabot on the shoulder. He turned to see Champe and Morse Hazel, the latter Champe's straw boss, a man who had never been accorded the status of foreman at the Five Bar because that would have necessitated more money. However, Champe paid Hazel regular wages on time and without argument, two facts which gave the straw boss position.

Champe looked Cabot over with a grin. "You sure he's the right one, Morse?"

"Sure he's the oldest Sexton kid, ain't you, button?"

"Yeah." Cabot kept watching Champe.

"Morse says he's been hearing a wild rumor — something about your old man trying to sew up all the hay in the Agate Valley." Champe studied Cabot insolently. "Is that right?"

"Ask my father."

The false good humor faded out of Champe's expression. "You've made quite a step up from a plowboy, I hear." Champe looked at Cabot's pistol, at the range clothes that had come from Belknap's commissary. "Sparking one of the old he-sow's girls, too."

"What do you want?" Cabot asked. He didn't like this standing all alone, with the room growing quiet.

"I asked you a question, kid. What's this story about your old man trying to corner the hay?"

"Ask my father."

"You just ain't much on politeness, are you, kid?"

Champe shook his head. The mock regret of the gesture, the meanness in his eyes, this deliberate baiting, were all part of dishonesty, an unfairness that shocked Cabot. But he wasted no time on moraliz-

171

ing; his mind went ahead to the next step.

Champe was trying to start something. Maybe at first he had wanted only to insult Cabot and make him talk, but the affair was deeper now. *He shoots people,* Cabot thought. *He's used that pistol to shoot men. If he tries anything with me I'll shoot him first.*

"I'm going to ask you one more time about that hay, Sexton."

"I told you where to find out."

"Doggone!" Champe said mildly. "You just ain't polite, kid." He lashed out suddenly with the back of his hand and knocked Cabot against the bar.

Cabot's eyes watered from the snap of a knuckle against his upper lip. He tasted blood. For a moment he leaned against the bar, blinking his eyes, surprised.

Champe grinned. "What about the hay?"

Forgetting all about his pistol, Cabot put one foot on the rail to raise himself. He kicked Champe in the belly as hard as he could. The rancher grunted as he staggered back. Morse Hazel started to swing on Cabot. He stopped, frozen in an awkward position, when Rusty said, "Put the fist away, Hazel." Rusty's pistol was half drawn.

Hazel stepped back. Champe straightened from a stooped position, getting his breath in great heaves. Cabot saw the high intensity of his wrath then, the happy wickedness that drove him into shooting men over something as simple as a request for wages earned.

"I'm giving you the chance to draw," Champe said.

It was that or the ignominy of begging off. Cabot was afraid, and then the fear was gone. He had to shoot a man or be shot.

"Champe!" The voice snarled with command. "Leave that kid alone!"

Champe's eyes slid to the side and then fixed on Cabot again. "You don't figure in this, Irv."

"I said leave him alone. He told you where to get your information, if you've got the guts to do it."

Cabot saw the change in Champe, a rage that almost carried him into his move, and then a calculation, and then a fear that crumbled everything. It was done, Cabot realized, when Champe turned to look at Irv Stalcup, still seated at the poker table, both hands in sight.

"Just because you had bad luck with Sexton," Champe said, "is no reason —"

"I didn't try to jump one of the pups, Champe. I went to the old wolf himself."

"I heard what happened to you, too."

"Keep talking," Stalcup said, "and I'll take it you want to start something with me. Do you?"

Champe's rage was all directed toward Cabot then. The rancher turned away from Stalcup's challenge and went back to the bar. Not looking at Irv, he said, "I'll have to remember you interfered, Stalcup."

Irv said a word that held a world of contempt.

Champe did not answer, and the brittle temper of the room was once more soft. Rusty poured another drink and said, oblivious of the Five Bar men near him: "Champe always did pick his turkeys mighty careful. This time he made two mistakes."

Maybe he did pick his turkeys carefully, Cabot thought; but there had been no consideration for that idea in Cabot a minute before when a pistol fight had been just a wink away, and he had been scared to death. He looked across the room at Irv. Ugly, with skin that lay on his face in burned plates, with a brutal vitality in every gesture, Stalcup caught Cabot's glance and returned it with a stare that said nothing.

Frank Belknap came in the front door.

174

His presence caused a small check in the flow of noise. He came toward the bar with the awkward walk that contrasted oddly with his general precise bearing. In passing Cabot and Rusty, he gave them a sharp glance and said nothing.

Belknap's clothes were dusty. A seam on one of his hip pockets was coming loose. During the last few days at the railroad, under the pressure of work, he had not shaved. There was a toughness about him that Cabot had never observed before; but when he thought about it Cabot knew it was not the outer changes that gave him the impression.

Old Belknap, in spite of his speech and odd little ways, was as much a man as anyone in the room, Irv Stalcup included. The idea pleased Cabot.

Rusty gulped his drink. "Let's slope out of here," he muttered. "I'm on probation already, and even if you are the boss's fair-haired boy it wouldn't help either of us a damned bit if we run over that half-hour Tracy let us have."

They went outside. Cummerford was riding down the street. He stopped when he saw them and waited until they mounted and came up to him. "You got about two minutes left," he said.

"If I'd knowed that," Rusty said, "I'd had three more drinks." He rode on with Cabot. After a moment Cummerford turned his horse and followed them.

"He meant that half-hour, all right," Cabot said.

Rusty gave him a quick look. "Yeah, but that ain't what brought him in. He made a mistake letting you stick your nose toward trouble, and Belknap told him so. That's what brought old Frank in. Did you see him look at us as he walked past? Belknap thought you might be in grief, so he came in to see about it."

"He didn't have a pistol on."

"He's got more guts without a pistol than most men with one. Irv didn't have no pistol either, but he told Champe what to do." Rusty grinned. "You're a popular boy with old Frank, Cabot; but if you ever try to take advantage of it he'll cut you down to size so fast you'll be mumbling, 'Who would have thunk it?' "

"I ain't figuring to take advantage of him or anyone else," Cabot said. Wanting to marry Belknap's oldest daughter was not being unfair. But since Cabot had been at the K he had seen Helen only once, and then she had been just distantly polite.

She was sore because he had cut her

short that day he picked out the horses. And then there was her mother, too, to consider. Suddenly Cabot was as full of troubles as any mortal man in love can be.

"You and me will never set high with Jim Champe," Rusty said. "Give him the right chance, and he'll plug either one of us. Don't think he can't get the job done, either. No matter what kind of front we put up back there in Lew's place, we're both prime turkeys for a bastard like Champe."

Chapter 9

The snows of early fall lay in patchwork on the north slopes. In the timber where the sun on its shortening daily sweep across the south had little chance to work, the snow was uniformly four inches deep. If the normal weather pattern held, there would be more snow, and then thaws in January, and thereafter the range would be reasonably open.

With fierce intensity John Sexton fought a personal battle against there being a normal weather pattern; he was hard to live with and he knew it.

Earlier than he had expected he saw Belknap coming to take his first contracted hay. Working on the woodpile, Malcolm and Roman saw the racks on Little Johnny hill, miles away, and set up a clamor. The racks halted inside Sexton's south line fence. Belknap rode in alone.

At once Sexton tried to be brisk with business, but Belknap put him off politely when Moira invited the K owner inside for coffee. Belknap relaxed and was pleasant, answering Moira's questions about his family. He mentioned that Cabot was driving one of the hayracks.

Sexton grew restless. "I'll go on down to where your crew is. You'll be along in a minute?"

"Of course," Belknap said.

Roman and Malcolm were already with their brother. There were five racks and a crew of K cowboys, who were looking with glum resignment at the chore ahead.

One glance at Cabot and Sexton knew the boy had gone across the dine into manhood. He fitted in with the men around him.

Sexton asked, "How do you like it over there?"

"Fine." Cabot nodded. He was neither sullen nor triumphant in his little victory.

"I could use you here this winter. There may be plenty of work."

"You'd have to pay me," Cabot said. "That wouldn't be fair to Roman and Mac."

He was right, Sexton knew; and long ago Sexton had been right, also, when he left home. But still he cast around for some basis for a quarrel, remembering that

Cabot had defied him when he walked away.

Sexton might have found his reason but Belknap rode up then. "Where do you want us to start, Sexton?" Belknap eyed the fenced stacks with a sharp expression.

"Down at the old Renault place, Belknap. How much do you want right away?"

"Three hundred tons — but not from the Renault place. Our agreement was that the hay came from here."

"What's the difference?" Sexton asked.

"The agreement said here. You will recall what I told you of my father saying that grass from this end of the valley —"

"Yeah." Sexton had forgotten Belknap's slavish belief in every casual remark his father ever dropped. He scowled at his stacks. Every yard was tightly fenced, but the hay on the Renault place was in open fields. "I don't want to tear down fences."

"The agreement said the hay would come from here."

"Take it then!" Sexton turned away angrily and his glance fell on Cabot. "You might say hello to your mother, if you can spare a few minutes."

"He will have the time," Belknap said evenly.

Sexton knew then that Belknap and Moira had spent a few minutes talking about Cabot. He turned the buckskin that he had selected for himself at the K some time before, and rode away. He went past the house and looked at it resentfully, and then set out, aimlessly at first, toward Mexican Ridge. After a half-hour he knew where he was going.

Fall-stripped aspens were bleak on the site of the old trading post, but from the place Sexton could see to the wastelands east, clear into the dry, worthless country south of Nelson, and he could look beyond the hills where Belknap's house was folded into its small valley. The sharp Maderos stood grimly to the west. A turn of his head and he could look upon the great barrier of the Sawatch Range.

But he was not interested in looking up; he kept gazing out toward the K, which lay below him.

This was the place for a house. The breezes in summer would be cool, and in winter the black timber that started at the falls of Agate Creek would break the sweep of the wind.

He would build a tremendous house of the red stone that lay in even ledges on the head of Agate Creek. From the deep wide porch he could gaze out and say to Frank Belknap, "There's your place down there, somewhere in those hills."

Mary would have loved it here.

The air was cold when he rode back to the farm at dusk. Moira had kept his supper warm. He was full of plans about the new house, but something in his wife's quiet attitude made him hesitate to tell her.

"Where's the boys?" he asked.

"They rode over to Belknap's on the last trip with Cabot. They're going to visit there tonight."

"You let them do that!"

"I did. You've worked them like hired men lately, John. They'll be back tomorrow."

It was all right, after all. Let them see how the Belknaps lived; then they would have more interest in what Sexton planned to do. Sure, it was all right. He told Moira about his plans for the great house on Mexican Ridge.

"That's Stalcup range, John."

"It's open ground, like 90 per cent of the range here. I've got homestead rights I've never used. In the spring I'll file on that land and hire the house built. You'll have to go up there with me sometime. It overlooks everything down this way."

"I know. It overlooks this valley too."

"Of course. It makes this valley look like nothing."

"That's what I'm afraid of. This is where you belong," Moira said. She began to gather up the dishes.

"A man belongs as high as he can go."

"A castle on top of a mountain is built to hide the fear of those who live inside."

"Don't you want something better than this house?"

"Of course, someday."

"I'll get it for you sooner than that." Sexton sat back against the wall and watched Moira washing the dishes. The lamplight was soft upon her. She moved with the grace of a strong, mature woman. She finished her work and Sexton said, "Come here."

She stood beside him. He pulled her into his lap. "You're as beautiful as the day we were married."

"John, will you give up your idea of standing above all others in this land?"

"Don't you want me to be big? Don't you want all of us to have things we've never thought possible?"

"Yes, if all that comes from anything but ruination of someone else, and if it comes from yourself and not from the madness that's been in you since — for a long time."

Sexton laughed. "You're imagining things, Moira." He kissed her and there was no response. She was beautiful and she was in his arms. He kissed her again and there was no resistance and no response.

"Damn it, Moira! You've been like that for weeks! That's another way you're fighting me. I can take you. You're my wife and don't forget it!"

"Yes." She spoke without emotion. There was a sadness in her eyes, but behind that Sexton saw the hellfire of a challenge that warned him off.

He slept that night in Cabot's bed and in the morning he cursed himself for being weak; but at breakfast, when he looked at Moira, he knew he had not been weak: he had been soundly defeated.

The jolting hayracks came and went. When one stack was gone it was barely apparent. The whole process was wasteful and costly, Sexton knew. Baled hay would have simplified Belknap's work, but there was still a much better way than that.

He mentioned it casually when Belknap

came again at the end of the first week's hauling. "Did you ever think about bringing your cows to hay, instead of the other way around?"

"I have." Belknap offered Sexton a cigar. "If it becomes necessary, what arrangements will you offer?"

"I'll figure thirty pounds of hay per day for every cow you send over, your men to do the feeding. Hay will be three dollars a ton."

Without expression Belknap studied Sexton. "Long ago I should have bought at least one ranch in this valley. Frankly, if I had known in time that Renault wanted to sell, I would have bought his place."

"Didn't Jase Purdy tell you about it?" Sexton smiled.

"No. He offered me, on behalf of Allen, a hay contract at two and a half a ton, fifty cents under your price. I told him I wasn't interested, since I'd already made an agreement with you. I discovered later, of course, that Allen figured on buying the Renault place."

"But at the time it was a money-saving offer."

"It appeared to be," Belknap said coolly, "if a man wanted to break his word. To get back to the original subject: if I board

185

cattle here for three months, say, each cow will cost me approximately one-fifth of the present market value of the animal."

Sexton nodded.

"With no disrespect for my father, I still must say that he overlooked something here. I too am guilty. The practice of letting cows forage for themselves may prove costly in the long run. There will be a day in the West, Sexton, when the range won't be what it is now.

"Right now there is a new breed of cattle that is superior to the shorthorn as a beef product — the Hereford. In time I may change to them. Others will too, I'm sure. Then this valley, with the summer range on the mountains, will make an ideal combination."

"I see." Sexton's mind was spinning ahead.

Belknap kept his men hauling from dawn to dark. He hired all the racks in the valley, persisting in his stubborn principle of wintering his cows on his own land. He hauled five hundred tons before he stopped, delivering them a check for the full amount, with a deduction for three saddle horses.

Sexton went alone to Nelson. Before he took the train to Cottonwood he picked up a pair of cowboy boots he had ordered from Emil Siber. They pinched a little, but he liked the expensive look of the hand-tooled leather.

He smoked cigars on the train and pumped some vital information out of a hardware drummer who had taken him for a cowman.

Compared with Nelson, Cottonwood seemed like a city. There were twenty-seven saloons, and the whole place had an air of bustling activity that quickened Sexton's appreciation of business. In time he would be well known here and men would pay deference to him.

He made his first stop in a barbershop where a morose, bald-headed man went to work without any small talk.

"Who's the biggest grain-and-feed dealer here?" Sexton asked.

The barber took ten seconds to think about the question, "Joe Grayson." That was all he had to say until he let Sexton out of the chair and said, "One buck."

Sexton looked at himself in the mirror. The barber had done a good job on his stubborn hair. He liked the odor of bay rum and the clean look of his face. *I'm younger than I've been giving myself credit for,* he thought.

He came from a clothing store in a gray

broadcloth suit and a new gray hat with slightly upcurled brim. It was a conservative style of hat, the clerk had said; all prosperous cowmen were wearing them this fall. Sexton lit a cigar.

Two women passed. He saw them glance at him from the edges of their eyes, and after they had gone a few doors down the street they paused to look into a store window, once more slanting their interest back at him. He was pleased. He squared his shoulders as he went up the walk to find Joe Grayson.

The hay-and-grain dealer was a big untidy man with a corncob pipe in his mouth. His eyes were mild blue, his jaw most blunt. "Sexton?" His grip indicated that he could toss around a few of his own sacks of grain. "You one of them new Texas fellows from the Rosebud Mesa?"

"I'm from Nelson."

"Oh? I know Frank Belknap over there. Fine man." Grayson kept sizing Sexton up, as if puzzled because he could not associate him with a big outfit.

"What's hay worth?" Sexton asked.

Grayson's manner stiffened. "You got some to sell, you mean?"

"I might want to buy some."

Grayson led the way into an office that

was also the scalehouse. He slid a weight to zero on the beam and motioned Sexton into a homemade chair. "Baled native is five and a half a ton. Five even in hundred-ton lots, do your own hauling." Grayson watched teamsters loading oats from a warehouse beyond the scales platform outside.

"I want an option on twenty thousand tons." Sexton watched Grayson come around with a startled expression that slid quickly into a bargaining look. Carefully, as he had seen Belknap do, Sexton licked down the wrapper of his cigar. "Baled native, delivered in Nelson, at five dollars a ton."

"It can't be done." The feed man sat down on the corner of his desk. He was wearing an old black sweater, streaked with chaff, with holes in the front as large as whisky glasses. "You're a little low, Sexton."

"The price is all right." Sexton had learned a great deal from the drummer on the train. "At that figure you still make money, figuring freight and all."

"On twenty thousand tons . . ." Grayson seemed to be figuring. "All I've heard so far is something about an option. I haven't sold one bale of hay."

"Maybe you never will — to me, but I'll

give you five hundred dollars cash today for the option. Any part of the money I don't use in buying hay is yours."

Grayson's face was shrewdly set. "An option for how long?"

"Until May 1st, next year."

A teamster drove a load of oats onto the scales. Grayson weighed him out. He started to turn away and then ran the weight back to zero and stood staring at it. "You've got more hay around Nelson than anybody ever will need, Sexton."

Sexton put five hundred dollars on the desk. "I'm gambling. You can't lose, any way you look at it."

Grayson glanced at the money. "We could have a bad winter here too, come to think of it. That's your gamble. I could take a flyer here, if I wanted to."

"You sure can. Go ahead. I don't care whether I have your hay or not. All I want is an option binding delivery of the first twenty thousand tons of hay that goes to Nelson to me."

"I guessed that from the first." Grayson nodded. "You're putting up five hundred dollars for me not to sell hay in Nelson to anyone but you. I'll go that far, but I won't sign anything that forces me to deliver hay."

"You won't have to ship one bale," Sexton said. "But you will have to earn part of that five hundred. I want you to sew up the market here, so that anybody who wants hay will have to go through you."

Grayson frowned. "What makes you think it'll be a bad winter?"

"I'm gambling that it will, that's all."

"You've got your own hay, haven't you?"

Sexton nodded.

"All right. I'll go with you. I'll work the little hay growers here against each other and tie up what they got. The big outfits don't sell much anyway. They use most of it during the winter."

Little people against each other . . . The thought twisted unpleasantly through Sexton's brain; but this was business.

He went with Grayson to a lawyer and they had their agreement tightly drawn. Afterward Grayson bought the drinks, and Sexton wondered if he had thrown away five hundred dollars. But he was going all the way. A man made it big when he played it big, and fell when he backed away cautiously.

He had supper at the Winchester House. The waiters were attentive, and the other diners eyed him with no more than normal curiosity. He doubted that Joe Grayson, who was one of the leading merchants of the town, ever came here to eat, or that he would fit if he did come.

At the cashier's desk he bought a handful of fifty-cent cigars and wandered out to see the town. In the Golden Burro the dance-hall girls were attracted to him at once. There was also the prospect of a brawl in the scowls of two drunken miners and a group of cowboys who did not seem to like the way their partners sloughed them off to make a play for Sexton.

Already in his mind he had achieved a position that did not allow fighting in a hurdy-gurdy place, so he went down the street to the Teller Grand Salon, which was the Golden Burro again, but with a gaudier interior and more decorum in its employees.

He was considering dancing with a hard-faced blonde and buying her beer at a dollar and a half a throw, when he saw a small dark-haired girl coming down the great cherrywood stairway. She was a shaft of brightness in the noisy room. She moved with a gay lightness that caught all of Sexton's attention in an instant.

A red-faced man who looked like a drummer stepped out to intercept her, offering his arm. She brushed past him with a smile. She was in the middle of the floor when the shock struck Sexton.

Mary.

Great God! She reminded him of Mary. It was appalling; it verged on sacrilege. The girl came closer. She smiled at Sexton. He turned and went toward the bar, almost colliding with a waiter hurrying toward tables with a tray of drinks.

Sexton stared at a glitter of glassware and polished wood that took no form or meaning in his mind. A bartender, brisk and courteous, said, "Yes, sir?"

For a while Sexton did not comprehend the question or the purpose of the man who asked it. Then, harshly, he said, "Nothing, nothing," and the bartender moved away.

What tortuous extension of the imagination could have thrown his mind back to the little girl who had looked like her mother? Laughter came from the dance floor, trailing threads of ghostly mockery across Sexton's mind. He felt old and out of place.

After a time he went slowly back to watch the dancers. The dark-haired girl danced by in the arms of a tall, well dressed man. She was as graceful as a bending willow, but there was a blankness in her face, a lostness like the expression of a fallen angel.

Mary? No! Mary could never have been like her.

But Sexton was still shaken. The hard-faced blonde came up to him, smiling. He shook his head at her vaguely and walked out of the place.

A thin-lipped man in a black coat was idling by one of the posts of the wooden canopy outside. As he turned to look at Sexton, his coat brushed the post and revealed the wink of a marshal's badge on the flap of his shirt pocket.

"Where can a man have some fun here?" Sexton asked.

The marshal glanced at the building Sexton had just left. "You want to gamble?"

"No."

The marshal studied Sexton's clothes. He glanced down the street toward the railroad station. "Goldie Manners runs the kind of place you might be looking for, mister."

Shortly before the train was due to leave on its midnight run toward Nelson, Sexton came out of Miss Manners' establishment and paused to light a cigar as he looked toward the station. He gave no attention to people moving past until a man said, "Hello, Sexton."

Dr. McRae, his medical grip in his hand, was abreast of Sexton. He went on past before Sexton said, "Hold up, Doc; I'm heading to the station myself."

They walked along together, not speaking. Sexton looked with dislike on the dimly lighted coaches waiting on the siding. A group of cowboys were finishing a bottle before boarding the train. Sexton saw a bearded man handing children up the steps to where a woman received them and herded them into the car.

The man went up the steps with the last child clinging to his neck. When the light from the coach doorway struck him he looked like old Wes Hillers, who had fought under Berdan with Sexton. The resemblance created another ghostly shock. Old Wes had been killed at Chancellorsville, near a crumbling iron foundry on the first day.

Suddenly Sexton's cigar had a foul taste. He flipped it away. He looked at McRae. "Well, Doc, have you got any fatherly comment to make?"

The doctor gave him a tired look. "You flatter yourself, Sexton." McRae boarded the train.

Sexton went into the station to get a ticket. The sight of his own money reminded him that he should have bought some gifts for Moira and the boys. Cabot had always wanted . . . No. Cabot was no longer at home. Well, when Sexton got back he could give Moira and the boys some money and they could go to town and get what they wished.

The bulging gut of the big iron stove behind him threw heat on his new clothes and brought out the odor of strong perfume. He expected the old man across the counter to sniff and make some sly remark, but the ticket agent counted out the change and stamped the ticket and said without interest, "You'll get there at 5:03 A.M."

Sexton stood outside for a while. Bitter cold air was rolling off the Maderos. He hoped it would blow away the scents that rankled in his nostrils. He saw McRae leaning back wearily in his seat, his eyes open. The doctor looked as if he had just met a defeat and was too tired to do anything but wonder about it.

When the conductor called, Sexton walked across the cinders and got into the next coach behind McRae. The bearded man who had looked for an instant like

Wes Hillers was there with his family.

No, he didn't look much like old Wes at all, on close inspection, but Sexton went on past him and into the last coach. There was no one in it that he knew and no one who reminded him of anyone he had ever known.

Chapter 10

Meadow grasses still curled above the foot of snow that lay in Meldrum Park. The aspen thickets held no secrets now, for a man could look deep into their leafless barrenness. Beavers still slid in and out of a few holes in the ice of the huge ponds, but winter would level even those before long.

Belknap's shorthorns were foragers that knew how to paw. Five hundred of his strongest cows were here.

Riding the edge of the park with Cabot, Rusty Nichols said: "What happened with you and Helen? You ain't gone near the ranch since —"

"Nothing happened."

"All right. Nothing happened. Excuse the hell out of me, kid."

Cabot watched the cows digging for their food. Belknap was making a hard retreat, but before long he would have to move the herd farther south to the bare ridges, and then, as winter progressed, closer to his home place. In normal years feeding was a minor problem, for by the time his herds had been allowed to drift close to his home meadows, spring was opening up Belknap's range again.

But this was not a normal winter, even in Cabot Sexton's short stretch of memory.

Rusty saw the buckskin coming before it broke from the aspens at the lower end of the basin. He stopped his horse, grinning as he pulled his skullcap lower over his ears and turned the collar of his sheepskin up.

"That's Helen!" Cabot said.

"I do believe so. I hate to see things neglected, but I suppose one of us will have to ride down and see —" Rusty watched Cabot's horse start away briskly. He laughed when he saw the snow flying from its hoofs.

Cabot went in with a rush. His mind was full of a song and all his feelings were lifted. He rode close to Helen and stopped, looking for changes. They were nothing. Her freckles had faded, perhaps; there had been a leveling of the color of her hair because the sun was no longer strong.

He saw all the remembered things that could not change: the way she sat her horse, the poise of her neck and shoulders, her smile, the way she looked at him from under her dark brows.

He took a deep breath and said, "Hello."

"Hello, Cabbie."

They lived the full moment that only the young in love can know, when all is new, when experience is lacking to qualify the wonder of love with doubts.

Across the frozen meadows Rusty was singing, and his voice came faintly, clearly.

After a time Cabot said, "I can make some coffee."

Helen smiled. "My mother said for me not to go inside." Thereupon she swung down and went into the kitchen. Cabot put the horses in the lean-to beyond the wood-pile.

The coffee was a gesture that thumped upon the stove and could not make its presence known to the young people who stood with their arms about each other. The few soft words that are wondrous magic came to them, and Cabot knew that no one had ever felt as he did then.

Helen said, "I found out what my mother said to you that day."

"It was all right. She was nice about it." The words were easy, but the truth of what Mrs. Belknap had said was still with Cabot. A romantic moment could lift him high, but the strain of realism in him was too strong to let him live on exalted dreams. He did not know it, but he had become a full-fledged member of an adult world.

"My father says I don't have to go away to school."

"That's fine." It *was* fine, but Cabot glanced into the room beyond the kitchen, where he and Rusty slept. The rest of the house they had never entered after the first day they came here, but it was there, a reminder that Helen had everything and he had little hopes of having anything for years to come.

Dreams were great and love was wonderful, but even if Mrs. Belknap's arrows had not gone deep into her target Cabot would have realized what he knew now.

"You don't sound like you mean it." Helen gave him the same precise, inquiring look Frank Belknap wore when he delivered a question.

"I'm thinking that we don't want to wait years to get married, but what else can we do?" Cabot shook his head. "I can't take anything from your father, even if he offered it. Your mother is against me. She —"

"When she loses," Helen said, "she loses gracefully. She goes completely to the other side when she knows she's lost a point. I know my mother very well."

"Yeah." Cabot had his doubts. "Suppose I can keep this job working for your father. Then what would we do if we got married — move in with your folks?" He shook his head again.

The girl went across the room and moved the coffeepot. "Your father bought the Renault farm. Lease it from him. We'll raise cattle and horses."

"There's no market for horses, Helen, and cattle are about fifteen dollars a head. You've got to have a thousand square miles of range —"

"Bunk! My father has two thousand square miles of range, and there are times when he has to borrow money to pay his crews. If he didn't think his own father had been next to Christ when it came to good judgment in all things, he would have pulled his horns in long ago and started raising better cattle on a smaller scale."

Cabot stared. Before, he had noticed but never observed the practicalness in Helen. Rather than lessening his feeling for her, it increased it.

"I've got twenty horses of my own to start with," the girl said. "We'll sell most of them, if we have to. We can start with cows, that new breed that my father is afraid to try because his father never heard of them."

"I've heard him talk of them." Cabot felt better. There was a direction to move in, and he should be able to find some way to start. "Cows first, and then we'll build up to where you can play around with horses."

"It won't be playing around, Cabot. There's a market for good horses, once you've got the reputation for raising them."

"I think you're right." Cabot now had a solid appreciation of this girl he loved; it was like discovering that something bright and beautiful is also highly useful. He grinned suddenly. "That Renault place has bedbugs."

"I don't doubt it. We'll fumigate the living daylights out of it before we ever move in."

Cabot was amazed to know that the thoughts of a bedbug campaign could hold such a delicious appeal.

When they went outside Rusty was riding in, a bulky figure in his sheepskin. Helen waited to say hello to him before she left. Watching her buckskin kicking snow toward the lower end of the park, Cabot said, "We sure have been having fine weather."

"I know what you mean." Rusty looked at the sky. "But before dark it's going to snow like hell."

The sky, indeed, was the color of an old bullet, and the Sawatch Range was blotted out. "I'm going home," Cabot said. "I'll be back late tonight."

"Belknap won't like it if he finds out. When he says stay with a herd, that's what he means. Don't think he ain't watching the weather. We'll probably be moving —"

"I'll be back tonight."

In a murk of falling snow Cabot missed the trail on Spanish Mesa. All about him the huge flakes were slanting into the aspens like ghostly smoke, whispering against his clothes, sliding down to wet his saddle, melting on the shoulders of the buckskin.

He blundered into a maze of gulches in the cedar brakes and there he saw a few far-wandered Stalcup steers. When he hit the old Gunnison mine on Forsythe Creek, he knew where he was. He had lost an hour by veering that far south, and time seemed most important.

Riding across his father's stubble fields, he saw one stackyard fence after another. As the stacks, close huddled in the night, came drifting up to him, there seemed to be no end to them.

Light from the house reached out but dimly even after Cabot was in the yard. He passed a snow-covered cone that puzzled him until he realized it was the woodpile, three times larger than he had ever seen it before.

Everything was warm and unchanged inside. His mother smiled and hugged him. His father shook his hand and gripped him by the shoulder, and his brothers tumbled out of bed to greet him.

The withering fibers of the youth he had been so shortly before called out to all of this, and for a time it was as if he had never left in anger, but there was no sadness in the knowledge that he would never live here again.

When the immediate questions had been answered, Cabot began to see changes in his parents, a determined quietness in his mother, restraint and hardness in his father. All his life Cabot had seen them as a pair, a combination of authority, of love and understanding; now they were two distinct people, careful not to stir in his presence some disturbance that lay between them.

Mrs. Sexton said: "Roman, back to bed with you and Malcolm. You can jaw with

Cabot in the morning."

Malcolm fidgeted beside Cabot's chair. He acted as if his oldest brother's presence gave him some assurance that had been lost. John Sexton cut harshly through his wife's repeated order: "Get to bed, Malcolm. I won't tell you again."

The violence of his father's tone startled Cabot. But still Malcolm hesitated, hanging on to Cabot's chair. "You're sure you'll be here in the morning, Cabot?"

"Sure I will, Mac."

"Promise?"

Malcolm had the strong Sexton build, and his face was developing toward the hard, spare lines of his father's features, but still there was much of his mother in his expression now, and all at once so much of Mary that Cabot felt a catch in his throat. The boy's appeal brought back poignant remembrance.

"I'll be here, you knothead." Cabot took his brother under his arm and carried him into the bedroom and dumped him, laughing, on his bed. "Go to sleep."

Cabot turned to leave. He saw his father's boots beside his old bed and his father's sheepskin thrown on a chair beside it. He lifted one corner of the pillow. His father's nightshirt was folded under it.

"Roman's got a girl," Malcolm said. "Harriet Belknap. He thinks she's —"

"Shut up," Roman said.

"Both of you." Cabot went out and closed the door. His father had the living-room door open and was looking out on the storm, smiling.

When Cabot looked directly at his mother he knew she was reading his face.

Sexton closed the door. He paced around the room, still smiling. He stood at the fireplace a few moments, rubbing his hands, and the light on the hard planes of his features revealed an intensity that made Cabot glance once more at his mother.

"How much hay is Belknap feeding now, Cabot?" Sexton asked.

"I don't know. I haven't been near the K home place for six weeks."

"You'll be a damned sight closer soon. You won't be holding cows in Meldrum Park after this storm." Sexton turned his back to the flames, shoving his hands under his belt, standing there with his feet solidly set. "Altogether, Belknap has got a thousand tons of hay from me. He hasn't used much of it yet, I figure, but he's got it. Already three of the little ranchers from way out east have been up and down the valley trying to buy hay."

"You wouldn't sell them any?" Cabot felt a sick anger. Out east the range was poor. This much snow would lock it tight.

"Why, of course," Sexton said. "But they wouldn't meet my price."

"You've got hay you'll never need."

"It will be needed, and when it is they'll pay for it — or go without." Sexton's voice was savage. "You're like your mother, Cabot, when she harps on that subject. A cow runs wild and the owner scarcely sees it. It grows up on public grass and water and the owner sells it for fifteen dollars.

"I raise my hay on land I bought with money that came from sweat and an aching back. I dug ditches, watered it, cut it, hauled it, stacked it — and then in an average year, if I'm lucky, I can get three dollars a ton for a few stacks. This year, by God, I'll do better. I'll get back something for my years of work. That's all I want, and there's nothing unfair in it."

"You lie," Mrs. Sexton said quietly. "You've got a hatred in your soul that has nothing to do with money."

Sexton ignored her. "You can see my point, Cabot."

Cabot saw, instead, parents that were strangers; the shock left him cold clear through to the spine. He saw a steady hatred in his mother and a wildness of purpose in his father. No matter how logical his father's view had sounded, there was a lie in it. John Sexton had never been a man to try to fatten on the woes of others. The change was frightening.

"I know the work involved in raising hay," Cabot said slowly. He paused to say what else he had in mind.

"You see, Moira! Cabot understands, even if you refuse to. I want you back home, Cabot. I'll pay you, and I'll need you before the winter is over."

Moira said: "That pistol troubles me, son. I wish you'd take it off while you're in this house."

"I'm sorry. I forgot." Cabot hung his pistol belt on a rack with two others near the door. He glanced across his shoulder at his mother, wondering how his father had beaten down her objections to having weapons in the room.

Sexton said, "I've got a chance this winter to make some money, Cabot. If you'll —"

"Cabot didn't come here to talk about hay, John," Mrs. Sexton said. "He has his own affairs, I think."

Cabot laid his plans out then. He saw his father nod occasionally and he saw a happy intentness in his mother as she listened.

"Where will you get these cows you're talking about?" Sexton asked.

"I'll find out from Belknap when the time comes."

"How will you pay for them?"

"Borrow the money somewhere — at the bank, I guess."

Sexton grunted. "You lease ground from me, with the idea of buying it when you can. I don't own all the Renault place you understand, but I can handle Glinkman. He'll go along with me, I know. You borrow money for your stock. It won't be from Allen, but there's ways to find it." He nodded "It could work out, even the part about the horses."

Cabot was not sure why but he had expected difficulties from his father. "Then you'll let me have —"

"I'll talk to Glinkman. I'll get things straightened out with him. Yes, you can have the Renault place. That is, if you'll come work for me the rest of the winter."

Mrs. Sexton said, "No!"

"Be quiet, Moira." Sexton had another look outside. The lamplight died just beyond the door in the thickly falling snow.

Breakers of cold coursed along the floor and made the fireplace throw smoke into the room. After a time Sexton closed the door. "How about it, Cabot?"

Cabot thought of bellowing, starving cattle, of fences around haystacks, of angry men who would not let their cows die just because John Sexton willed it. His father was wrong, but still Cabot thought he should help him. Perhaps the January thaws would solve the problem, after all; and in the spring Cabot would have a lease on his own place.

Embers popped in the fireplace. Snow hissed against the windows and scratched faintly on the door.

"Let him have his start without tying him down to your quarrel," Mrs. Sexton said.

Her husband shook his head.

"Then don't take his offer, Cabot. The stink of dead brutes and the smell of human blood your father would spill this winter will make the odors of the wedding bouquets for your wife if you listen to him."

Sexton's voice trembled. "Be still, Moira!"

The prophecy struck Cabot hard. It raised the mystic in him for an instant. He remembered the feel of stories his mother had told him long ago, of strange curses, of misty things on the moors at night. But he was hardheaded. The disturbed look he gave his mother smoothed away when he realized she was merely speaking truth as she saw it.

It was truth for Cabot too. Helen would know that he had sold principle for expediency. Frank Belknap, with his strict ideas about integrity, would recognize the fact instantly. What mattered most was that Cabot felt the same way himself.

The Renault place was gone; there would have to be some other plan. Cabot thought of the bleak ride back to Meldrum Park.

He looked at his father. "No."

"Why not?" It was accusation.

"You're trying to make money from misery. Because you're my father I may have to help you, but I won't be bribed into it."

Anger gritted in Sexton's tone. "Let Belknap lease you land then, if you think he's got any that's fit for what you want. I intended to give you the Renault place after I saw — To hell with it." He turned on his wife. "I told you to keep still, Moira. You had to —"

"I made up my own mind," Cabot said.

"Like so much hell you did! If she had kept —"

"Never mind." Cabot threw his will across the path of his father's anger, and then he realized he was willing to hurl physical force too, if it was needed.

With a stark expression Moira watched, seeing two John Sextons in violent opposition, two men carried beyond reason by the grinding of like personalities.

She said, "That's enough."

Sexton still watched his son. "The whelp is telling me what to do in my own house."

"I got out of your house once," Cabot said. "I'll stay out, except when I want to see my mother."

"I need no protecting, Cabot," Moira said.

Sexton strode to the fireplace. With his back to his son he said, "Get out now!"

"I will." Cabot went to the pistol rack.

The door of the boys' bedroom banged open and Malcolm stood there in his nightshirt. "You promised to stay, Cabot! You said you'd be here in the morning."

They knew then that Malcolm had been listening all the time. Cabot and his father glared at each other with mingled shame and anger. Mrs. Sexton went quickly to her youngest son. "He's going to stay, Malcolm. He promised, so he's going to stay all night."

213

Once more Cabot thought it was hatred he saw in the look his mother turned on Sexton. But when his father broke, Cabot got the impression that the giving-way came from within and not from any outward influence.

"Stay then," Sexton said. "You'd be a fool to tackle that ride tonight." He walked away into Mary's bedroom.

When Mrs. Sexton returned from putting Malcolm to bed, Cabot was still at the pistol rack, holding the belt he had started to strap on. His mother came to him and put her hand upon his shoulder. With the other hand she took the belt and hung it back on the rack.

She smiled, and Cabot watched her narrowly, wondering if she was trying to coax him, as if he were a child. "The pair of you are just alike. He hasn't really changed, Cabot. Not yet he hasn't. Remember that, son."

It was not a false smile, or a grimace of self-pity. Cabot saw in it everything his mother had to bear, and the courage she could bring to the task. His anger of a moment ago seemed childish now. He knew, also, that he had not seen hatred in her eyes against his father, but condemnation of his father's acts.

"This started the day Mary died," Mrs. Sexton murmured. "He won't let himself forget and I don't know how to help him."

Remembering Mary and his own loss, which he had not spewed out in bitterness against others, Cabot was miserable with too much understanding. But he knew the men his father was trying to squeeze would understand no more than what was happening to them.

"Should I come back, like he wants me to?"

"I don't know whether my advice is good or bad, Cabot, and so I'll give no more of it." Mrs. Sexton turned away. "Sleep in your old bed tonight." She went to the room she no longer shared with her husband.

Snow was still falling when Cabot rode away the next morning. When his tiring buckskin broke down through the timber into Meldrum Park, he saw Belknap and Cummerford and a half dozen riders already organized to drive the herd from the snowy basin.

He went straight to Belknap. "I had to go home last night. It was important."

Belknap nodded soberly. He removed his hat and knocked the weighting snow from it. In the brief time of the act snow fell

215

thickly into his close-cut gray hair. "Your orders were to stay here. Now I must discharge you."

Cabot stared his anger. *What a stinking deal!* He saw no regret, no anger in return, but a firmness that stood like a mountain.

"You can go back to the ranch now, or you can help us take this herd to Cosslett Meadows."

After a time Cabot said: "I'm here. I'll help."

It was a miserable chore. The snow stopped and a cold wind ran. The horses wallowed and the herd was contrary. At dark the riders pushed the bunch into Cosslett Meadows, where the outer perimeter of the storm had dropped a little less snow than higher up.

Belknap had a camp here and a few haystacks. Barely enough hay, Cabot estimated, to last until the herd was rested enough to be moved again.

Rusty's face was dark with cold. "You're lucky you got fired before the hay-forking starts."

"I wouldn't have minded."

"Going back home?"

Cabot shook his head.

"Old Crowley was looking for a livery hand last time I was in town. Don't know whether he landed one."

From the meadows Cabot rode on to the K with Belknap and Cummerford. Neither had much to say, but Cabot did find out that Mrs. Belknap and the girls had gone to Cottonwood for a week.

In the dead of night the three men reached the ranch and got down stiffly. Linneus Carrothers came out to take care of Belknap's horse. Carrothers sized up the situation. After Belknap was gone he said, "Well, they come and go here, especially the young, smart ones."

Cabot had a hot reply on his tongue, when Cummerford said, "You're one that's been here too long, Linneus."

"I'll be here when you're gone too!"

Carrothers had been answered. Cabot went to get his pay. Belknap wrote him a check in the paneled office. The K owner did not say that he was sorry or that his rules were made to apply to all. He was like a bloodless magistrate. He paid Cabot off and told him that the cook was getting coffee and hot sandwiches prepared.

"Let *me* tell Helen about this," Cabot said.

"Of course."

Belknap offered his hand. Cabot shook it. All the way to the cookshack he was puzzled by the thought of how simply he seemed to have accepted his firing. But he knew that he had not taken it easily; there was a bitterness that would be stronger tomorrow.

In fairness he could not blame Belknap; but if his own father had acted decently, being fired would not have been one bad blow heaped upon another. Cabot at least would have had a lease on the Renault farm. Now everything was failure.

The bleakness did not go away the next morning. He could not see any farther into the future than he could see toward Nelson through the skating gusts of snow. It was much colder than yesterday.

He rode away through the trampled pastures where it appeared that Belknap already had most of his cattle. A feeding crew was scattering hay behind a rack, with bellowing cattle streaming after the wagon like minnows after bread crumbs.

Cabot headed the buckskin toward town. He went over the first ridge and was lost in the long white swells of the hills. The wind pelted him.

Chapter 11

Out of the northwest raced white spindrift that skirted down John Sexton's fields and shrieked against his dark-topped stacks of hay. He lived then with grim anticipation. When the wind lifted and the weather showed bare signs of breaking he lived angrily, afraid of being betrayed.

Then a foot of fresh snow fell. The wind resumed. He was happy again, except when he saw Moira's dark look upon him.

Big Will Stalcup rode up the valley. Sexton met him in the yard and felt the first fierce twistings of revenge when Will said, with an air of false heartiness: "You got our tails in a split stick, Sexton. I'd like to talk to you."

It would have been better if Irv had come, bucking the snow, crawling in out of the wind, begging. But Irv was not that kind.

His brother tried not to be as he drank Moira's coffee and let the warmth of the house melt the cold from his bones.

219

Will was an indecisive man and he was no fighter, but he said what he had to say with a certain dignity. "We're going to be ruined, Sexton, if you don't help us. It's too late to try to haul hay. We'd like to save what we can by wintering on the Renault place." He hesitated. "Glinkman is for it."

"He would be," Sexton said.

Sexton's coldness flustered Will. He looked at Moira in frank appeal. She said nothing.

"We understand you made an offer to Belknap to winter some of his cows," Will said.

"I did."

"That was on this place, I heard."

"Yes."

"What's your offer to let us feed at the Renault ranch?"

This was the high, fierce moment that Sexton had waited for. He said, "Half the cattle you bring there."

Will laughed easily enough. "One thing I like —" He stopped when he realized Sexton was serious. "Good God, Sexton!" Will's eyes bulged. His face was loose suddenly, as if he had been shocked physically. "You don't mean . . . You . . ." All the handsomeness sagged out of him.

Sexton nodded, grinding out a savage pleasure from the moment. Too bad it was not Irv.

Will got up slowly. "This is a hell of a thing for me to carry back to the ranch."

"Irv could have come himself."

"Don't think he won't," Will said, "but not to beg." It was not a threat, but a statement, and Will appeared to deplore the fact that it was true. He turned to Moira. "Thanks for the coffee, Mrs. Sexton."

"Won't you stay for dinner, Mr. Stalcup?"

"Thank you, no. I'll — I'll be getting along."

Sexton rubbed a clear spot on the kitchen window and watched Will riding north toward Mexican Ridge. The wind bristled around him. He stopped once to adjust his cinch, and then he stood for a few moments looking at a fenced stackyard. He rode on slowly, head lowered against the drive of snow.

"The man came here in all civility," Moira said. "His brother knows that he came." She left the implication for John Sexton to develop as he would.

"To hell with the Stalcups!" Sexton was frustrated, for all at once he could no longer derive any great feeling of satisfaction from watching the lonely, defeated figure bowed against the wind out there. But of course if it had been Irv . . . Irv was the one who had refused all help the day Mary was dying.

"John," Moira said, "what can I do to help you?"

The question went so deep into Moira's understanding of him that Sexton was afraid. "Just leave me alone," he said. "Keep still and leave me alone!"

"You are pitifully alone," she said quietly.

"God damn it! If you —"

Malcolm and Roman came in then from cleaning out the barn. Their entrance forestalled another quarrel.

Sexton stared at the place he had rubbed clear on the glass; it grew opaque once more, and he heard the wind rattling snow against the pane.

He had three more visitors within the next two days. The first two were Mort Howell, deputy sheriff, and Lew Glinkman. Sexton smiled bitterly when he saw them riding in together. Both of them were getting ready to run. He knew what was in their minds even before he helped them get their horses out of the cold.

Once inside, the two of them could

scarcely get their coattails three feet from the fireplace. They talked about the weather for a while. Glinkman kept smoothing the white wings of his hair. At last he said, "John, I want to get clear of the Renault place."

"All right. Get the papers ready and I'll come in and pay you."

"They're ready now." Glinkman pulled some documents out of his inside coat pocket. Howell witnessed the signatures and Sexton paid cash for Glinkman's one-half interest in the Renault place.

Sexton said, "You said once some folks would still remember it was you who put up the money in the first place, no matter if you did drop the deal later."

"I know," Glinkman said. "It's the best I can do now. You're on the wrong track, John."

No matter what Glinkman said, Sexton could not get mad at him. The man was scared and Sexton found excuses for him. Anything Glinkman did was all right with Sexton.

Now Mort Howell had to come around to his business. "You're breeding trouble out here, Sexton," he said. "How much help are you figuring from the law?"

Sexton smiled. "None." He spoke in

such a flat, insulting tone that Howell turned red.

"I'm trying to uphold the law," Howell said. "You know your property is going to be invaded, and I know that I can't stop it, not altogether. I'm trying to plan something, because I know I'm not going to get any help from Cottonwood.

"There's some things you could do to help me, Sexton. In the first place, I wish you'd move your family out of here. The next thing, I hear you're going to feed some of Belknap's cows, maybe — I wish you'd put them on the Renault farm. You're not very well fenced down there, but if Belknap has cows on the place nobody's likely to try to crowd in."

No indeed, Sexton thought, not with Tracy Cummerford and a few other of Belknap's men around. Howell had a point. Sexton gave the deputy new appraisal.

"How about it, Mrs. Sexton?" Howell asked. "Will you move to town until —"

"No thank you, Mr. Howell," Moira said.

Howell studied her an instant. He sighed and turned back to Sexton. "About the Renault —"

"No good, Howell. If Belknap has to

224

bring his cows to hay, he'll want them here. He thinks this is better grass than farther down the valley."

"Better grass? Hay is hay, and in the dead of winter, if your cattle are starving, what —"

"That's Belknap's idea," Sexton said. "The ghost of his father does all the talking for him."

Howell looked again at Moira. "Mrs. Sexton, I wish you would —"

She shook her head. Trapped by the curious cross currents of human behavior, the deputy shook his head too. "Well," he said, "I've had a nice cold ride for exactly nothing."

"Don't worry," Sexton said. "Just stay close to that big heater in the station. You'll be all right."

Howell turned red again. "I intend to do what I can, even if you're making it rough sledding." He bowed to Moira and went out into the cold, holding the door so that Malcolm could enter with an armload of wood.

"I'm running, John," Glinkman said. "I ain't too ashamed to admit it."

"I understand, Lew." Sexton thought he did understand.

Glinkman gave him an odd look and

went out to ride away with Howell. The wind enveloped them with white as they broke anew the trail they had made shortly before.

Moira said, "Lew Glinkman can't do anything wrong, as far as you're concerned, can he?"

"He was the only outsider who helped me that day."

"Then you do realize what's driving you?"

"It's not what you think at all, Moira. I want to amount to something. I want to get things for you and the boys. I want —"

"Give Cabot the Renault place, if you're so set on doing something for the boys."

"You twist my words around!" Sexton complained. "Cabot wouldn't help me. Why should I help him?"

They were back on the spinning circle of their disagreement.

Irv Stalcup was the third visitor. He rode in on a frost-rimmed black gelding and swung down in the yard without invitation. His face was cold-chipped red and white. He stamped around the yard, beating his hands together, sizing up Sexton with a mixture of respect and arrogance. Moira came to the door and invited him inside. Irv touched his hat and said he guessed he wouldn't be around long enough to bother.

The boys rubbed spy holes on the living-room window and peered out intently.

"You and me had our personal troubles, Sexton," Irv said, "and maybe we'll have some more one of these times. You made me back away once and you licked me once, but that ain't worrying me a bit. You didn't get no virgin either time." Irv rolled his burly shoulders and beat his mittened hands together.

"You could say I was a little wrong once, about the water, but now you're so damn' far off, Sexton, that nothing out of the past matters." Irv paused. "The offer you made Will was the talk of a fool."

He was finished, stopping so abruptly that Sexton thought there must be a thought uncompleted. There was: Irv was leaving the way open for bargaining. It had to be galling him, no matter if he had stated himself in an insulting manner.

"What's your proposition?" Sexton asked.

Irv would not be drawn out to be smashed down and laughed at. He said, "I'll hear one from you."

You could not cat-and-mouse with Irv Stalcup. He had made his approach. If he had swallowed any of his arrogance Sexton could not detect the fact. Sexton was angered by his own frustration. Revenge was eluding him. "The offer I made Will is the only one you'll hear from me."

"All right." Irv took it as he was taking the wind, as if it had no force to disturb him. His breath whipped past the ragged cape of his mackintosh. His cold-tortured features stared at Sexton a long moment, and then Irv swung up in the saddle. "Use your head, Sexton, and get your family out of here."

"Thanks for the advice."

"I gave it. Remember I did." Irv's lips were twisted away from his teeth as he looked down at Sexton. "We could have done better, you and me."

Irv Stalcup rode up the valley. The cape of his mackintosh lifted and made him appear humpbacked. His black horse crashed into the wind and snow with powerful strides.

I turned away the last chance for peace, Sexton thought. He glanced toward the house, and then went down to the barn.

Jim Champe returned from Cottonwood with a wickedness roiling in him like sand in a muddy river. There was no hay to be had unless a man bought it from Sexton. That, Champe would not do. Being held up was bad enough, but being outfoxed by a farmer was more than Champe could take.

Rankling worst of all was the knowledge that he could have cornered hay himself. He just had not thought of it. God damn Sexton; he might make a fortune.

Champe came down the coach steps and viewed Nelson savagely. It was a little after five in the morning, bitterly cold, with light just touching the hard-packed street and upcurving piles of snow against the dead buildings. The hotel showed a dim light.

A man could have made a fortune. The thought ate like acid.

Champe buttoned his sheepskin and went toward the hotel. He had an evil hangover and a grudge against the world. Looking across the street at the Sundown, he thought, *There's the greedy bastard who put up the money to wreck me.*

Morse Hazel and four men of Champe's winter crew were in the hotel. It enraged Champe to see them in warm beds. He kicked them out, cursing. Hazel, a gaunt man whose tie to Champe was more stupidity than loyalty, yawned his breath into the cold room and began to dress.

He asked, "Where's the cars of hay spotted, Jim?"

"There ain't no cars, you damn' fool! Get back to the ranch and drive everything that can walk to the Renault place."

"That'll take some doings," Hazel said. "We're spread all over the rock country clear to —"

"Shut up and move! Don't loaf around town for breakfast. I got troubles enough without any arguments."

One of the cowboys said: "I got troubles too, Champe. I ain't been paid for two months."

Champe's eyes glinted wickedly. "You'll get your money, Thurman."

"How about now?"

Champe drew his pistol. "Yes, you'll get paid right now if I hear one more word out of you." Temper made him uglier than Irv Stalcup could ever be.

Thurman had no more to say. He dressed. He started to roll a cigarette, and Champe slashed it from his fingers. "I told you to get moving!"

Having run his crew from the hotel, Champe went to bed.

Hazel roused Cabot Sexton, the livery hostler. The Five Bar men had brought in one hayrack and made arrangements to

230

hire wagons. Hazel ordered Jack Thurman, the cowboy who had protested about his pay, to drive Champe's rack home, with his horse tied behind it.

When Cabot tried to collect the livery bill, Hazel told him curtly that Champe would pay. The Five Bar riders started out of town. They left Thurman lumbering through the snow far behind with the rack. He went less than a quarter of a mile before he turned around and came back to the livery.

"I just quit a job," he told Cabot. "Do whatever you want to with this team."

Cabot sized him up and wasn't sure that the man was worth anything or not; but he said, "You might try my old man for a job."

"I might," Thurman said, and went away to find breakfast.

Jim Champe got up in an evil mood. The hotel owner insulted him by making him pay for his breakfast, instead of putting it on account. He knew Crowley would be laying for him, too, when he went to get his horse from the livery. A penny-grasping bunch of townsmen.

He went to the Sundown and had a couple of drinks. It was too soon after breakfast, and they didn't lay well on his stomach. He kept looking at Lew Glink-man's soft, pale face and getting angrier all the time.

"Lew, after all the money cowmen have spent in this place, you served us a filthy trick when you jumped in with Sexton on the Renault ranch. Ain't it about time you tried to get right on that deal?"

"I have already, as far as I know how."

"Oh?" Champe said with suspicion. "What did you do, lease to Belknap or Stalcup?"

"Sold my half out to Sexton."

Champe cursed shrilly. "Why didn't you say you wanted to sell! You and me could have worked out some deal."

"I imagine," Glinkman said dryly.

"What do you mean by that?"

"Don't try to pick a fight with me, Champe. As soon as I knew what Sexton was up to, I didn't like it any more than you."

"The hell you say! You knew what you were up to, all right, but when things started to tighten down you got scared and tried to get out. You loaned the money in the first place, Glinkman. That makes you guilty as hell of trying to ruin us all!"

Glinkman sighed. He had known that was the way his part would be interpreted.

Champe was in one of his foul moods, ready to kill. Glinkman didn't want any trouble with him.

The saloonman was taking verbal abuse, and wondering with sick helplessness why he didn't have the courage to lean across the bar with a bung starter and hit Champe in the head, when Mort Howell, Rusty Nichols, and Jack Thurman walked in. Champe gave them a bitter look; he knew what was coming.

Howell said, "Thurman here says you owe him two months' wages, Champe."

"I paid him before he went to Cottonwood."

"You lie," Thurman said. "I want my money."

Champe sized them up. Howell was not armed but the other two were. Champe glared at the deputy. "So you're siding in now with drunken riders that blow their wages and cry that they wasn't paid."

"The man made a complaint," Howell said.

Champe laughed. "The man lied. Morse Hazel can swear I paid him."

"I imagine," Howell said. He turned to Thurman. "See what I meant? Your next move, if you want to take it, is to go to court."

Thurman was a compact, round-faced little man. His headshake as he stared at Champe showed a complete lack of faith in court proceedings. "No, I won't do that."

"You better go sweep the station out, Howell." Champe laughed, but he watched both Howell and Nichols narrowly. He did not like this surprising set-up a bit, and he was jarred to know that Howell had guts enough to face him.

The three men went out. Rocked into semi-civility for a moment, Champe said to Glinkman, "What the hell has got into Howell anyway?"

"Nothing. Nobody paid any attention to him because nothing important ever came up to test him. Maybe he ain't as heavy as some, but he'll try to do his job."

"Where does Nichols figure in?"

"He got fired at the K. He was buying a ticket to leave when Howell made him a deputy."

Champe thought there was sneaking satisfaction behind Glinkman's words. It infuriated him. He said: "Glinkman, you cowardly little scut, you're the one that backed Sexton up. You're a dirty, stinking —"

"I don't want no wrangle with you." Glinkman's face was pale red. "Just pay up

234

and leave the place."

"Come around the bar and collect it." Champe had several more drinks. He tossed a half full bottle on the floor and walked out. A crawling bunch of scared townsmen, that's what they all were. He stood on the walk watching the scudding wind on the sage flats east of town. His range was buried. There wasn't enough grass in the rock country to last a hundred cows a week.

The greasy-sack ranchers over there had already tried to argue about his right to run cows in the piñon country. Ent Tucker had suggested he try to drive to Morgan River. A hundred and twenty-five miles across wasteland, with little chance there would be enough to graze on the Morgan to winter the survivors of the drive.

It was Agate Valley or ruin.

The whole thing was John Sexton's fault; and behind Sexton was Glinkman.

Cold began to soak into Champe. The whisky he had drunk poured foul vapors through his mind. He stared at the livery for a few moments and then tramped toward it, leaving his sheepskin unbuttoned as the snow blew against his shirt.

The acrid warmth of the big building enveloped Champe. He stood by the closed door of the office until his eyes adjusted to the gloom, and then he went toward the figure forking manure through a window at the far end of the stalls. Cabot Sexton was wearing his pistol as he worked.

Champe said, "What's the idea of leaving my team in the cold end of this place?"

Cabot leaned on the fork. "Those were the only stalls we had. You knew that when —"

"I'm tired of taking lip from you, Sexton. Either you move that team or —"

"They stay right where they are, as far as I'm concerned. See Crowley if you don't like it."

"Uh-huh." Champe was happy now. He felt fine. Cabot Sexton made a clear, clean target with his back against the light of the window.

The office door creaked open at Champe's back. Judge Crowley stepped out, with a huge pipe in his teeth and a shotgun in his hands. "Pay your bill, Champe, and then maybe we can listen to your complaints about where your horses ought to be."

With his hand poised above the butt grips of his pistol, Champe sucked in breath with a shudder. Everything was going wrong. The whole miserable town was in league against him.

"Part of your bill runs back to last winter," Crowley said. "What do you say you step into the office here and settle up?"

Champe's eyes were narrow and wicked as he turned away from Cabot Sexton. He snarled over the bill Crowley presented, but in the end he paid from a money belt that bulged with cash from his fall shipping.

Afterward he went to the Rangeview, and by mid-afternoon he was so drunk a bartender disarmed him. Three men helped him to the hotel and dumped him into bed. His body was almost helpless but his mind was still writhing.

In the dead of night he woke up. Snow drifted against the window near his bed looked faintly blue, and he could see out on the sage flats to where the horizon, frosty with stars, met the frozen earth.

After a time he dressed and went outside. A light engine was chuffing in the yards. A lantern showed in the switchman's shanty, but the rest of Nelson was dead under the clutch of cold and night.

Champe went to the back door of the Sundown, drawing his heavy clasp knife on the way. The oak bar across the doorway would have stopped a runaway steer, but the door itself was only an inch and a quarter thick, and the age-cracked panels, where they tapered into the stiles, had hardly any thickness at all.

Using two hands on the knife, Champe cut out a top panel. He reached in and lifted the bar, and presently, shading a match in his hands, he was standing in Glinkman's storeroom.

When he left, black smoke from the coal oil of a spilled lamp was mingling with the blue flames of burning whisky.

From the upstairs window of the livery, on his way back to bed after quieting a horse that had put its leg through the slats of its stall, Cabot saw the tall man crossing the street. He was sure it was Champe, but Champe had been dead drunk when they hauled him away.

Cabot watched the man go into the hotel, and then went back to his own bed and fell asleep a few minutes later.

Champe, too, was actually asleep when an excited clerk began to rouse all guests. The clerk told Howell afterward that it had taken a lot of effort to rouse the man, and that he had been almost helplessly drunk even then.

The wind was out of the northwest. It

seemed stronger now that it had work to do. A bucket brigade grunted and sweated while water they spilled upon their clothes froze quickly, and the water that went upon the flames meant nothing but that men had a will to fight. Shadows danced grotesquely and the snow was red.

It was a wide street and that was all that saved the side where the hotel stood. Beaten back, the fire fighters shoveled snow on embers that carried across the street, while owners of threatened buildings stood on their roofs and threw water from buckets that they raised and lowered with ropes.

Glinkman's Sundown went in a crackling hurry. Soon afterward the bakery was gone, and then Mrs. Thom's millinery, the World's Fair Café, Peterson's gunsmith's shop, and Greenberg's hardware store.

Under Howell's direction men dynamited two vacant buildings, and then dragged the walls and heavy framing members across the street with ropes and horses. This action saved the lower end of the street. Allen's bank and mercantile was the last to go.

Before sunup there was ruin between Judge Crowley's office and Siber's saddlery.

Looking at it, his pale skin blistered, his white hair singed, Lew Glinkman smiled wanly. "I won't have to fool with that sink drain one more time," he said.

Champe watched the fire from the inside of the hotel. For a time he was awed by what he had done, but that wore off and then he was sorry the flames had not jumped to the livery and roasted Cabot Sexton alive. Damn all Sextons. There would be other days to deal with them.

Lew Glinkman, at least, had been paid off good, and in a measure, the whole miserable town. Champe started home when the fun was over. He rode a mile before he returned to the fact that his own situation was as bad as before. The wickedness roiled up again, edged now by the fear that someone might trace the destruction to him.

Chapter 12

John Sexton accepted the fact that his fences would be cut, that cattle would be driven on his land. Knowing Irv Stalcup, he thought the open declaration of war would come in broad daylight.

That was the way it came.

The wind carried the sounds of the herd when it was still two miles away, a mournful bawling riding down the frosty air. Sexton nodded at his sons. "Come on."

Moira stood behind Malcolm, gripping him by the shoulders. "Not this boy, John. I will have something left out of your madness."

Sexton went with Roman to the loft of the barn. It was an arsenal, loop-holed on four sides, banked high against the sides with hay, and Sexton had stocked it with rifles and ammunition. He looked around him and knew how weak his position was. There should be at least four men below; but his neighbors down the valley had refused to help him, and his own son had refused to help him.

Roman kept trying to swallow. "What if they —"

"I'll tell you what to do."

The herd broke over the western ridge. Two big steers were churning snow in the lead. The Stalcups were on point, behind them four other riders. About three hundred head, Sexton guessed. The cows tried to scatter as they came spilling down the slope. In flurries of snow riders beat them back into line.

They passed close to the white fence on the hill. Sexton said, "Hand me my Sharps, Roman."

Careful to keep his breath off the telescope, Sexton peered through the tube. His eyes were cold. His face became as bleak as the heavy bar of iron. Irv Stalcup jumped into clear focus on the distant hill.

"You going to shoot?" Roman's voice wavered.

"Not yet. Don't get excited."

Irv trotted ahead. He got down and cut the fence, dragging the lower wires from the snow and hurling them aside. He mounted, and while he waited for the herd to reach the gap he stared down on the buildings in the middle of the white fields.

Cows streamed out on Sexton's land.

The riders let them spread and followed Irv's signal. Two men leaped down and cut the fence around a stackyard two posts beyond each side of a corner. Four ropes went out. The horses took the strain, and the sharp cracking of wood came to Sexton seconds after he saw the actual breaking through his telescope.

He made instinctive note of the time lag and it helped him estimate the range.

One man dismounted to free the ropes from the wrecked fence. His horse was a blood bay, cleanly dark against the snow. Sexton could see the vapor of its breath as he touched the trigger.

He shot the horse through the neck. Its nose hit the snow like a hammer stroke and then the animal was a bright mass lying on the snow.

Sexton moved along the banked hay to the next loophole, away from the cloud of pale smoke. Roman peered from a crack in the hay door, his mouth open. "Hey! That was an awful long shot! Did you hit where —"

"Get down!"

Roman dropped before the rifles replied. Bullets ripped through the roof peak. Others died against the hay. It was as Sexton had figured: over the distance there was no accuracy for ordinary long guns. He fitted the ponderous barrel of the sniper's rifle into the loophole before him.

Cows were pouring through the broken stackyard fence. The riders had gone behind the stack, but then a man ran out and began to strip the rig from the dead horse. Sexton watched him and let him scuttle back to cover with his saddle and bridle.

Then Irv rode into the open and pointed toward another stackyard. Two riders paused to fire at the barn before they followed orders. *Carbines,* Sexton thought with contempt.

When a man leaped from his horse to cut the wire, Sexton sliced a bullet into the snow close to him. The man dropped his cutters and ran back to the horse. Irv Stalcup's bellowed orders came faintly to the barn. He put his rope on the corner post, and two riders moved in to help him.

They were shaking out their stiff ropes when Sexton knocked splinters from the corner post with a careful shot. The riders hesitated, looking across their shoulders at the barn. Irv yelled an order. He flipped his own rope free of the post and took his men around the stackyard. Minutes later Sexton heard the screeching of wire and the explosive popping of a post.

Keeping under cover, Stalcup's men breached another stackyard. They cut the line fence near the southwest corner of the field and started back along the hill. One man was riding behind Will Stalcup's saddle.

Sexton took long aim and broke the foreleg of the horse. He knew it must have seemed like an incredible shot to the men on the hill. Two of them emptied their carbines at the barn. Again the distance and the walls of hay absorbed their accuracy.

Will was stumbling in panic toward his brother's horse. Irv's forcefulness stood clearly in Sexton's telescope. Irv drove his brother back to the crippled horse and made him take the rig and then shoot the animal with a pistol.

Two horses were carrying double as the riders quit their angling ascent of the hill and went straight up to get out of range quickly. Irv was the last to go away. He sat his horse in range of the sniper's rifle for a long moment before he followed his men.

Watching him, Sexton saw that Irv was not looking at the barn, but at the frenzied cows crowding into the stackyards.

This was only the beginning.

It was dusk when Sexton and Roman

245

gave up their efforts to drive all the cattle from the fields. They managed to push about half the herd outside the fence. Several times Sexton raised his pistol to shoot stubborn cows that broke around him.

But he had spent a lifetime raising animals and caring for them; even now, raging and weary, he could not force himself to shoot these gaunt, starved cows that kept crowding back for hay. In the morning . . . Tomorrow he'd clear them all out of here or kill them.

In the dusk the blood bay lay on its side with snow drifting against it. Sexton looked at it morosely as he and Roman rode past on their way back to the house. Sexton tried to tell himself that this horse and the one Will had been forced to kill were payment for the sorrel of last summer.

Moira had kept supper hot in the oven. She served it without speaking. Sexton ate with little appetite, wondering how soon the quarrel would start.

The boys went to their room, and he heard them talking in low voices. He was standing at the window when Moira said, "What now?"

The question pulled the trigger of anger. "I'll drive them out of here or kill them!"

"Starving brutes. Will they understand why they're dying?"

"You talk like a fool!"

Moira left him with his anger and his loneliness. Across the snow came the bellow of cows driven beyond the repaired fence. From the eastern hills a wolf howled, and then there was a chorus of them.

This was a winter made for wolves.

Sexton did not rest well. The bellowing of the cattle and the triumphant howling of the wolves disturbed him. The house creaked with cold. He heard Moira get up several times to put wood in the stove. He slept hard at last, and when he woke he knew instantly that something was wrong.

It was a feeling that came from knowing that something had happened a moment or an hour before, and that he had sensed it but not acted upon it. With a pistol in his hand he padded around the house. The boys were all right.

Moira was not in her room.

He dressed and went outside. He heard the crunch of snow and saw his wife coming in from the fields with an ax in her hand. There was defiance in the way she strode through the bitter dawn with her heavy skirts dragging the snow. She threw the ax toward the woodpile and came on toward the house.

"So you let them back in?"

"Yes."

Sexton saw frozen blood where wire had ripped her hand. She looked at him without fear. There was no defiance in her eyes, but a high courage that held his respect. And then he saw a silent pleading, a reaching out toward him, a plea based on the love of a lifetime between them.

It almost broke the knot inside him; but an instant later he saw, or thought he saw, pity. That he could not bear. Rage spouted high, through reason, through love, shattering anything that tried to block him.

"Moira, I have a right to beat you until you whimper for mercy."

John Sexton met a will as powerful as his own. "You have not," Moira said. "And never in anger touch me again." The quality in her was love of justice, man's only rightful claim to dignity.

"By God —"

Sexton's wife made him step aside as she passed him and went into the house. He heard the banging of stove lids as she went about her morning chores.

Suddenly heavy of limbs and with a weakness that left him trembling, Sexton crunched through the snow toward the barn to do his own morning work.

He was returning to the house when he saw the rider on the crest above Mary's grave, a man moving slowly in the cold blue light of early morning, hunched in his saddle like a sick Indian. He looked as if he had been out all night. Sexton watched him bear north, turn around a butte, and disappear.

Probably one of Irv's men. Sexton watched snow whirling from the ragged edges of the butte, white pennants above a land that moaned with winter.

Irv would be back.

There was no use to try to fight it out alone, with Moira against him, and Cabot refusing to help. Send one of the boys to the K to tell Belknap to bring his cows here. That would stop Irv, and then there would be only the Renault place to defend. Stubbornness kept Sexton from acting on the thought at once. Maybe Belknap would come without asking. Then it could not be said that Sexton had cried for help.

Sexton postponed his decision.

Brittle with cold, Bent Hunley, the rider Irv had left to watch the Sexton place, rode into the Circle Arrow before noon. Irv waved him into the cookshack.

"What happened, Bent?"

"Nothing." Hunley removed his sheepskin. Under it was a blanket coat, and under his hat a woolen shawl. He spread his hands above the stove. "They got some of the bunch run out yesterday. They fixed the line fence, but —"

"How many did he kill?"

Hunley shook his head. "It was a funny thing, Irv. He started to shoot cows several times. He never did."

"Not a single one?"

"No." Hunley turned his backside to the stove. "I was damn' nigh froze to death this morning when I heard a banging. I sneaked a look over the ridge and seen the woman down there trying to cut wire with an ax. She let them cows him and the kid choused out last night back into the field."

Irv gave his rider a craggy, brutal stare. "What did Sexton do then?"

"Nothing, not up to the time I left."

Irv cursed. He twisted away and tried to look through a steamed-up window. If Sexton had torn into the herd with bullets, it would have made things easier. Then this business about the woman coming out to let the cows into the field again. By God, she was a better woman than Sexton deserved!

Two good horses were dead. It could have been two or three men, the way Sexton handled that deep-belching cannon of his. Irv considered the fact. It did not change his mind; it merely gave him pause, for one of the few times in his life.

Irv Stalcup respected two things in human beings: great strength or great weakness. What lay in between was a gray, muddy quality that he held in contempt. Champe was a gray man. Irv's own brother was one. Most men in the world were, as far as Irv was concerned.

John Sexton was something else. He was a fighter. He gave fair warning of his intentions. Irv damned him for refusing to see reason, for Irv himself could see reason, after it had been beaten into him.

Hunley poured himself a mug of coffee. He made sucking sounds with his lips before they touched the hot liquid. "There's three deputies at the Renault place: Sexton's kid, Rusty Nichols, and Jack Thurman, the fellow that quit Champe."

A sort of wonder crossed Irv's ugly features. Mort Howell had not been fooling when he said he would deputize men. The kid would fight; he was his father's son, and he had been ready to take on Jim Champe with pistols. Rusty Nichols was a crazy cowboy with guts. Thurman — Irv did not know anything about him.

Still, nothing was changed. Irv had not even considered going into the Renault place by force. The challenge was at Sexton's ranch.

Stan Elwood came in. He was wearing a boot on his injured foot, trying not to limp. Irv flung a question at him like a lance. "What's your idea about Sexton, Stan?"

"He's a tough bastard."

"Tell me something I don't know."

"I got a grudge against him," Elwood said. "But I don't want to kill him."

"Why not?"

Muscles made little ridges in Elwood's loose skin as he frowned. "You were wrong about the water that started all this, Irv. I'll follow the same orders again, but you were still wrong."

"We've been over all that," Irv said sourly. "What matters now is twenty-five hundred head of starving cows." He stared at his foreman, a man he respected enough to try to understand. "I let Will try his way. It didn't work. Then I went far enough to try to talk to him myself.

"Yesterday I opened the pot to see if he'd

stay, and all the time I knew he was going to stay." Irv paused a moment, wondering why he had made any concession at all, once the lines were clearly drawn. "Now we'll run the hand out." He nodded, his lips tightly set. The expression of his will dominated the thoughts of those who watched him.

"Sexton or no Sexton, every head I've got goes into Agate Valley as quick as we can get the drive ready."

Elwood's face was stone quiet. He spoke slowly. "Suppose he makes his stand this time from the house, with his woman and the two kids there?"

"Then I can't help it."

Chapter 13

Tyrannized by the flow of time, Jim Champe rode away from the western ridges near Sexton's place late one day, followed in the blue dusk by the howling of wolves and the mounting plaint of dying cattle. He knew his own cows could not reach the valley sooner than two days from now, but he cursed Morse Hazel for being slow.

He went toward his camp at the old Gunnison mine on Forsythe Creek.

What had happened at Sexton's was clear. Two dead horses, a few Circle Arrow cows still in the fields, and many others drifting helplessly along the fences. The only puzzle was why Irv Stalcup had made a weak play to start. It was unlike him. But he would be back, and Sexton could not stop him the second time.

Let him have Sexton's hay. Irv could not complain when Champe went in on the Renault farm. Once established there, Champe could crowd up into Nafinger's or down into Lindstrom's, perhaps without too much violence.

There was a stigma attached to killing family men. Let Irv Stalcup take the weight of that. Hell was bound to pop from this affair afterward, but Champe could always hold that he himself had gone in on an uninhabited farm.

Mort Howell had placed Rusty Nichols on the Renault place, but that was nothing. One man was not going to stop Champe, who could say afterward that he had no idea of what Nichols' position was.

Cold bit at Champe as he turned toward his camp. His horse popped its hoofs through the crusted snow. A wolf cruised out from the stark aspens and stood an instant on a ridge, looking down at him with fire dripping from its eyes before it trotted north.

The uncertain factor was Frank Belknap. There were several ways he might upset affairs; Champe worried about them all.

His horse lunged up through the deep-drifted snow of the gulch and came at last to the old mine cabin, once a bunkhouse. Champe led the horse inside and began to break up more of the rotting floor for firewood. The stove was rusty, the pipe full of lacy holes, and until there was a good draft going, smoke leaked into the room and made the horse jumpy.

Champe gave it a bait of oats. He took provisions from a gunny sack hanging from the ridge log and cooked himself a meal that he ate without relish.

Cold poured through cracks where chinking once had been. The candle guttered nervously. The dead of winter and here he was in this stinking place, all because of John Sexton. Champe got a bottle of whisky from his sack. He drank, sitting on a three-legged stool near the stove, cursing the horse when gusts of smoke made it nervous.

By the time he wrapped his blankets around him in a rat-fouled bunk, he was nursing a blackness against the world.

In the middle of the morning of the next day he rode out to meet Morse Hazel, who was due with word of the Five Bar cows. He saw his foreman below the mouth of the gulch where the sage flats spilled out toward the Renault farm. Hazel was talking to another rider on a little pinto.

It looked like a kid. Champe rode closer. By God, it was a kid! The boy rode away when Champe was yet fifty yards from the meeting. He yelled, "Wait a minute there, son!"

The boy looked at him and kept going,

angling west, away from the valley.

Champe went in on Hazel angrily. "That was one of Sexton's brats, wasn't it?"

"Yeah." Hazel's face was cold bright, but underneath lay a grayness, as if the man were very tired. "The herd is on —"

"Where was he going?"

"The kid?" Hazel blinked. "He said to the K to stay a few days. The boys are bringing the herd —"

"You damned fool!" Champe said viciously. "His old man is sending him to Belknap for help. If Belknap gets cows in here before I do, I ain't got a chance."

"I never thought of that. I —"

"You never think of anything! Belknap has got all his cows right at his ranch. The sanctimonious old —" Champe sawed his horse around and went after the pinto.

"Don't — You can't —" Hazel followed Champe.

The pinto was working toward the hills. "Hey!" Champe yelled. "Hold up there, kid. I want to see you."

Malcolm Sexton looked over his shoulder and urged his pony into a trot. Champe roweled his long-legged dun into a run, and then Malcolm, still looking back, jumped the pinto into a lunging gallop. Hazel followed, uncertain of what

Champe had in mind.

The pony was no match for the big dun. Hazel crossed two hills and was on the crest of a third when he saw that Champe had almost overhauled the boy. Champe drew his pistol. The report was a heavy bark in the frosty air. Malcolm was knocked off his pony. The ends of a scarf tied around his neck streamed out. He struck in a burst of snow and lay there almost buried, motionless.

Champe shot again. The pinto humped and bucked. The next shot dropped its hindquarters. The pony pawed with its forefeet and then they began to skid out from under it. The horse screamed shrilly. It settled into the snow and lay there kicking.

Insane fury was still twisting Champe's face when he rode back to Hazel. The foreman looked at him with unabashed horror. "Jesus Christ, Jim. Jesus Christ."

"You fool! He was running straight to Belknap!"

Hazel kept staring.

"Come on!" Champe said.

"Maybe he — maybe —" Champe looked toward the pony. It was no longer kicking.

"God damn you! Come on!" Champe

drew his pistol.

"But maybe you didn't —"

"I know where I shoot!"

The pistol, and years of blind obedience, caused Hazel to turn his horse and follow Champe. But he still wore a stunned expression, and he kept looking back.

"Now, where's the herd?" Champe asked.

Hazel answered mechanically. "At Signal Post this morning when I left. They ought to be —"

"Stop looking back!" Champe's voice rose. Fear and revulsion were working across his face. "We're both in this, Morse, but don't worry —"

"Don't worry? My God, Jim —"

"Quit whining! He said he was going to stay at the K for a while, didn't he? Nobody will be looking for him. Tonight the wolves will be at the pony, and before daylight tomorrow we'll do something with the kid."

Before daylight. The thought made a horrible tightening in Hazel's mind. He said, "Maybe we ought to go back there now."

"No! I don't want to see him now. I don't want to look at him right now, you understand!"

Champe's voice broke. His face was terrible to see. Hazel recognized the truth: Champe was so badly shaken he did not have the guts to look on what he had done. He was stalling to build up his courage.

Hazel followed him; he did not know what else to do, but it seemed that distance would effect a miraculous disassociation from what had happened, and so at last he said, "I ought to go back to the herd."

"You stay with me."

They started up the gulch toward the Gunnison mine. Champe asked, "Did you cross near the Renault place?"

"Yeah. Pretty close."

"See Nichols?"

"All three of them," Hazel answered.

Champe swung around. "What do you mean?"

"Nichols and young Sexton and Jack Thurman."

"Did they see you?"

"I suppose. They were all coming from the barn."

Champe swore savagely, but his eyes narrowed down to a cunning glint. He had seen only Rusty Nichols when he sized up the house, and he was sure that Nichols had not seen him. He worked on the thought; it developed well.

He watched Hazel sharply after they

reached the cabin. The man was deathly afraid, and because some of the same fear was hooked into Champe he hated Morse Hazel.

"Where's your guts?" Champe asked.

Hazel was sitting on a bunk filled with the litter of a rat-chewed mattress. "I got guts for most things, but —" He stared at the floor. "He was just a little kid, Jim. He —"

"He was a Sexton brat, and he was running for help!"

Hazel had refused a drink before, but now he went to the shelf table where Champe had set a bottle. Hazel drank as if to find magic in the whisky to erase memory.

"Things will work out," Champe said. "Have I ever tackled anything yet that I didn't get out of?"

"I guess not." Hazel tried to build assurance from the thought. But a kid . . . just a kid with a scared look. Hazel saw him splashing into the snow and he heard again the screaming of the pony.

The candle blew out. Hazel leaped to relight it. Champe did not move, but his presence bore heavily on Hazel. When light wavered across the room again Champe was still staring at his foreman.

Hazel took another drink. He knew he might as well have been gulping water. Somewhere toward the valley a wolf called, a deep, savage sound rolling on the frozen land.

Chapter 14

By six in the evening it was dark. The three deputies in the Renault farmhouse had long before given up their card game, and now they were more tired from idleness than if they had been riding hard all day.

Rusty Nichols got up, yawning. "I still say, Cabot, you're trying to get us used to the smell of where we're all going someday." He sniffed the odor of sulphur candles Cabot had been burning off and on for three days to combat bedbugs.

Jack Thurman went to a dark window. He was a balding little man. Round-faced, his features were sprinkled with stiff, sparse whiskers. He reminded Cabot of an apple full of cactus spikes. "Now where did that damned Morse Hazel go?" he mused.

"He probably swung up the valley," Nichols said. "He's looking things over, that's all. By now he's headed back to the Five Bar to tell Champe it ain't no set-up down here."

"He still worries me," Thurman said.

"He'll do anything Champe tells him."

Thurman and Nichols went to bed. They cursed the odor of sulphur for a while and then they were asleep. Cabot sat with his feet on the oven door in the kitchen. He was relaxed in body but his mind was worried. He had talked to Helen in Nelson when she returned from Cottonwood. She was willing to run away with him to get married.

At the time the idea had seemed good; now it did not. He had talked, also, to Joe Allen about borrowing money to buy cattle. Allen had said maybe, if John Sexton or Frank Belknap would sign the note. Then Allen had been burned out and after that he did not want to talk to anyone about lending money.

That fire was an odd thing. Cabot was still reasonably sure he had seen Jim Champe in the street late at night; but he had heard the hotel clerk swear up and down to Mort Howell that Champe had been almost unable to walk when he was aroused, and that there had been no whisky in the room. So Cabot had kept his mouth shut.

The range leaked orange light into the room. Cabot listened to the creaking of the house, compressed by cold. It was not much of a house, but he and Helen could have fixed it up. The bitterness of that stirred him restlessly. He rose and put more piñon wood into the firebox.

Somewhere out on the lonely snowfields a wolf howled. The sound hung in Cabot's mind and made him vaguely uneasy. During the usual mild winters of the Agate country, wolves generally ranged lower, on the edges of the wasteland where deer and antelope herds browsed among the warm rocks.

Cabot turned to go to bed. He wondered if anything had happened yet at home. There had been no word, and he and the other two deputies had orders to stay right here, no matter what rumors came to them.

He was near the bedroom door when he stopped. It seemed that, faintly, he had heard a mewling somewhere outside. The Renaults had left a tomcat that still ranged around the barn, but this had been a kitten sound.

Cabot thought he heard it again. Then wind rattled against the house and he was not sure. He went to bed. He was dozing when he thought he heard the sound once more. This time it seemed like the yip of a coyote pup.

He pulled the blankets up to his nose. The room was cold. He had to allow that the odor of sulphur was not pleasant. He fell asleep. He jerked to complete awareness with a start some time later. Something hung in his mind, although the cause was no longer there. That damned sound again, he guessed.

He swung out on the cold floor and put his boots on and took his pistol from a chair beside the cot. The front door creaked as he opened it a few inches. Cold slashed his face. He looked out on a big chill land with frosty stars. Wind was raking brittle fingers across the crusted snow.

The hasp on the barn door was bumping against its staple; when the wind stopped the noise stopped. Cabot felt the hairs in his nostrils stiffening as he breathed. He was a fool for standing here in the rush of cold. He started to close the door.

The sound was clear. "Mr. Renault!" It was a ghostly, thin, mocking sound, crying the name of a man who had been gone for months. "Mr. Renault, please . . ." The voice ran away with a gust of wind, but the pleading note it left in Cabot's mind shocked him more than cold.

He walked out into the snow with the

pistol in his hand. In a drift, where the wind was mourning around the corner of the barn, he found his brother Malcolm huddled on his side. The coldness of his body as Cabot lifted him and ran toward the house was a shriek and a curse in Cabot's brain.

Near morning the wind died. The valley and the hills beyond were unbroken winter, resting under a faint blue light that gave beauty to the land. To Morse Hazel it was a ghastly land. He rode with Champe to do something about the body of Malcolm Sexton.

They found the place. Wolves slid away, standing on the hills to look down with molten eyes. After a time of tramping and kicking in the snow, Champe said: "He ain't here! You hear me, he ain't here!"

Hazel's relief was a mighty force, but he tried to hide it from Champe. "I guess not, Jim."

"You're thinking I missed him."

"I know better; you didn't. I seen it." Hazel watched the last wolf disappear. No, no! They would not bother a moving, living human being.

"We'll trail him," Champe said.

Hazel said, "Maybe —"

"Shut up! We'll trail him."

The wind had been working, but still there was the smooth dent of the boy's movements, and in the tall sage, a clearer trail. It was in the sage where they found the fresher marks of a horse, hard-ridden in the direction of the K. The boy's trail wavered on, but he had direction in mind.

It was getting daylight when, holding behind a ridge, Champe and Hazel looked down on the Renault farm.

"By God, he went there," Champe said.

Hazel nodded mutely. He wanted to run away; only Champe's watchful, vicious attitude held him. Both of them were rope meat now, Hazel was sure.

Champe kept staring down the hill. "Those horse tracks come from there. Somebody cut the fence to keep from going to a gate. Somebody went to the K, but now we've got as good a chance as Belknap to get a herd here." He looked at his foreman across his shoulder. "There's two men left there. We'll go down."

"They seen me yesterday," Hazel said, panicked. "If the kid's there, they'll think I did it."

"If he got there alive and talked," Champe said, "they know who done it." He hesitated. "I still got to go down."

"The kid's brother is there. They won't

give you a chance."

Champe knew he had to go. He had bungled once because he allowed some stupid emotion to overcome him. But there was still no certainty that the boy had made it to the house. Even if he had, blame might yet be turned on Hazel.

Hazel said, "You want me to circle around and go speed up the drive?"

Champe's look struck brutally into his foreman's fear. "Stay here. I'll signal you. Run, and this thing is on you for sure." Champe seemed to know what sprang in Hazel's mind, for he said, "Don't bank on me getting killed down there, Hazel."

Champe rode boldly down the hill. He went through the gap in the fence. The man who had cut it had left his pliers on top of a post. In the open fields where the wind had full sweep, there were no signs of the boy's trail.

No one challenged from the house. Champe then put the barn between him and the house and rode on. At the back of the barn he paused and kicked the manure window open. Jack Thurman's short-coupled grulla was the only horse inside. Champe rode into the yard and hailed.

He knew by the length of time that passed that he had surprised someone.

Then Thurman stepped outside, a pistol in his hand, his face forbidding.

"Put it away," Champe said mildly. "I admit I didn't pay you, Jack. I was drunk the day you braced me, but I'll settle up without a pistol on me."

"That's fine, but don't reach anywhere around your belt right now. Leave the money at the Rangeview."

"I will." Champe shook his head. "You don't have to keep that pistol on me. Hell, I know I'm covered from the inside."

Thurman was bitter, deadly, ready to kill. He did not relax, which was additional evidence to Champe that no one, except perhaps the boy, was inside the house.

The doubt about the boy was cleared when Thurman asked, "Where were you yesterday, Champe?"

The Sexton brat was here. If alive now, he had been unable to tell his story, else Thurman would not be hesitating by asking a question.

Champe said, "Where I was is none of your business, but I happened to be at the Signal Post camp until after dark. And then I had to ride all night looking for Morse Hazel. You see him?"

"I wouldn't say if I had."

"So I didn't pay," Champe said. "I will.

You don't have to hold that grudge forever. I was drunk —"

"Leave the money in town. Right now — ride on."

"I'm damned good and cold, Jack. I wish —"

"Go home and build yourself a fire."

"All right, all right! Being a deputy has gone to your head." Champe tried for exasperation just short of anger, both in his tone and in the way he let his next words trail away. "My God, Jack, you'd think I was —"

"Ride on."

"I'll tighten my cinch whether you like it or not." Champe gave Thurman no time to protest. He swung his leg over the saddle, banking that Thurman would not shoot in cold blood, gambling that he had confused the man's suspicions at least a little.

Champe drew his pistol as soon as the horse covered his descending body. He took one step and fired across the rump of the dun; Thurman was too late. Champe's bullet took him in the chest, driving him back against the door. Thurman's shot, all aim jarred from it, slurred into the snow. Champe shot him twice more in the chest as the man was sliding into a sitting position against the door.

Thurman's head dropped. The angle of the framing and the door held him. His wrists bent from the weight of inert arms against the snowy step. He bumped against Champe's legs, rolling on the threshold, as Champe opened the door and ran inside.

Malcolm Sexton was covered with blankets on a cot in the kitchen. His eyes were closed, his face colorless. Champe raised the pistol. His hand shook as he aimed it. But he could not pull the trigger. His mind at once found an excuse for what he thought was weakness: the kid was as good as dead already.

He put the pistol away and ran to a window. Hazel was coming down the hill in a trail of flying snow. That was all right; that was fine.

On the threshold Thurman made a low, moist sound. Champe did not look at him.

Wickedness was concentrated like awl points in Champe's eyes as he turned toward the cot again. He could not make the same mistake twice. But still he could not crash directly through his reluctance.

His eye fell on the lamp. He acted quickly then, smashing the glass tank on the woodbox. He used a piece of kindling as a taper, thrusting it into the firebox until it caught flame. He ran across Thurman's body and went to his horse.

Ferocity had warmed him. He reloaded his pistol while he waited for Hazel to come up. This time he would take no chances on a riding target. He wanted Hazel in the yard, on foot, and far enough from the house so that the flames would not touch him.

Hazel stared at the man in the doorway. "Jesus, Champe, that's Jack. What —"

"Sure it's Jack. He had the first shot."

The foreman saw the smoke building up inside. "The house is on fire!" He leaped down and ran to Thurman and started to drag him away. Another thought struck him when he saw that the deputy was dead. With horror on his face Hazel turned to Champe. "The kid? Is he —"

"He's not here."

Hazel saw the lie. He ducked his head and plunged inside the house. Champe heard him calling, cursing wildly. And then a few moments later Hazel came out, carrying Malcolm Sexton in his blankets.

"He's dead, Hazel. He was dead when I went in there."

"You lie, or you wouldn't have set the place on fire!" Hazel started toward the barn. He stopped and turned. "I'm through with you, Champe. You've made a liar and a fool out of me ever since I went to work for you. This finishes it. I'm through with you."

"All right. Go on. Take him to the barn, if you think he's alive."

Hazel took four more steps.

"That's far enough, Hazel."

Hazel took two more steps before his mind reached its final, full understanding of Jim Champe. Even then, he laid the boy in the snow instead of dropping him. He put him down and tried to make his draw as he spun to face Champe.

Champe's pistol was ready. It crashed across the snow two times. Hazel died a few feet away from the boy he had carried from the building.

The nagging of his first mistake was still a clawing at Champe's reluctance. He walked over and looked down at Hazel and knew there was no error there, but when he looked at the boy . . .

Malcolm was on his side in the snow. Wind was lifting the edges of the blankets that trailed around him. Superstition and terror tugged at Champe; this would be the third time if he did not make sure.

Once more he could not overcome some basic reluctance within him. He took one angry step in retreat and then wheeled around and came back. He started to reach down and feel the pallid face. His arm stiffened against the action and he jerked it away. Damn it, the boy was as good as dead, if he was not dead now.

Champe went across the yard to where Hazel's nervous horse had pranced away from the odor of smoke. He led the horse into the barn and left it there unsaddled with Thurman's grulla. Let that be one more item of confusion.

On the run Champe rode away, not looking at anything he had done. The kitchen wall of the house was burning, blooms of gray smoke bending down to run in streamers with the wind across the fields.

Riding to meet his herd, Champe had time to think about how murky some of his planning was; still, luck favored those who could brazen their way through, and he had always been able to do that, except at times when he had been forced to back down before men like Irv Stalcup.

Chapter 15

Frank Belknap considered all the moral aspects of the situation. This took him some time. Early in the morning Rusty Nichols had stumbled into the K, leading a horse with a pulled tendon, bearing a tale of trouble in Agate Valley. Someone, possibly Morse Hazel, had shot Malcolm Sexton.

The boy had crawled to the Renault place, where Mort Howell had stationed three deputies. Malcolm had been unable to tell what happened, but Cabot had jumped to the conclusion that his brother had been on the way to the K to ask Belknap to send help to John Sexton. The question was whether this was Cabot's idea or his father's idea.

It seemed to Belknap to be a delicate problem. It was not sound policy to help a man before he asked for help. Then, too, if he threw any considerable part of his crew across Irv Stalcup's path, he would be abetting downright extortion, which was what Sexton was attempting against the

Stalcups, and possibly against Jim Champe.

There was, of course, the offer Sexton had made to winter K cows at his farm. How much of that was honest and how much was based on a desire to ruin the Stalcups?

Belknap was bitterly opposed to being used. He sat in his office and tried to think things out.

His wife came in, heavily dressed. Belknap stared at the sheepskin-lined over-shoes; they made her look like a little bird with enormous feet. His eyes lifted to her face and he saw that the usual vagueness which she used as a weapon was gone.

She said: "Helen and I are leaving at once. She will take her horse so she can ride on up from the Renault place to tell Moira. Cabot will undoubtedly be at the farm with the doctor by the time we arrive."

Belknap nodded. "Linneus has the buggy ready. He'll drive you."

"Never mind Linneus. You may need even him before the day is over."

"What's that?" Belknap studied his wife's expression. When she made up her mind she was sharp and quick to act, and much harder to deal with than when she was fighting him with vagueness. He saw that she was clearly channeled down some line of action now. "What's this about needing Linneus?"

"You're taking men to Sexton's aren't you?"

"I don't know," Belknap said.

"You're afraid he's trying to use you against the Stalcups, aren't you?"

"Perhaps."

"He is, of course," Mrs. Belknap said. "He would be a fool not to. Your father did the same thing when he was fighting his way to control to what you have now. All men use each other."

"Never mind what my father did, Rose. My father —" Belknap saw that he was getting into a trap.

"You'll have to take your cows to Sexton's before long, Mr. Belknap, won't you? You'll have to —"

"Not just to block the Stalcups away from him. No. If I had known that he was going to hold up Irv and —"

"Bunk! Your conscience will be the death of you. Are you going to let your cattle starve?"

Belknap reached for a cigar. "Don't tell me how to run this ranch, Rose."

"I think I will. Your father's ghost has

run it long enough. I dare say your father would be appalled at your moral pussy-footing now, when a neighbor is in need of help that only you can give."

"The Stalcups are my neighbors too."

"They have no son who is going to marry Helen."

Belknap forgot to light his cigar. "What's that again?"

"They're planning to run away — Helen and Cabot. Do you think I don't have my ways of finding out what my daughters are thinking? Now wouldn't that be nice, to have them elope, throwing away the future that you and John Sexton could give them? I won't allow it, Mr. Belknap."

Belknap chewed his cigar. It was a habit he detested in others, but he did it now, silent, trying to adjust to his wife's change of views. Every now and then she reversed her line of thought so completely that he was left gaping.

Rose said, "In my opinion you made a silly error when you discharged Cabot."

"If you please, I'll run my affairs."

"If you please, I'll give you some badly needed advice, Mr. Belknap. It's one thing to have a policy and another to be pig-headed. You think of Cabot as a son. Yet you throw him out simply because he went home to see his father about leasing the Renault farm so that he and Helen could raise cattle there — that new kind that you drool over in your journal and are afraid to try."

Belknap tried to light his cigar. It would not draw. "They never said anything to me about that."

"Why should they? You set yourself up as the Lord in discharging Cabot. Now you're wiggling around, wishing you could make amends, but you're afraid to."

She was right, Belknap thought; but she was mixing this trouble in the valley into personal affairs, using it as a lever. She never would admit that she had ever opposed Cabot as a son-in-law.

Mrs. Belknap's pink face was flushed. She cocked her head. "Mr. Belknap, I've always suspected that you were somewhat of a rake before I met you."

"What!"

"Yes. A fast young blade." Mrs. Belknap sharpened her words on a tiny frown. "You must have made a bad mistake, or thought you did, so you've spent the rest of your life trying to be a gentleman. Now, by God, Mr. Belknap, let's find out if you're a gentleman or if you have any of your father's blood in you."

Mrs. Belknap left. Minutes later her husband saw her and Helen leaving in a buggy, towing a buckskin. Rusty Nichols was riding beside them. Yes, that was Rose, all right. She was like a religious convert, stronger in a changed belief than when holding the original one.

Belknap was a long time in making up his own mind. In the end it was not a question of what his father might have done, but purely a matter of what Frank Belknap was going to do. He moved swiftly then.

John Sexton and Roman came in from riding their line fences. About thirty cows were still inside. Snow-dusted carcasses lay close to the wire outside the west fence and some half dead cows were still on their feet, waiting for the wolves. The rest of the herd had drifted down the fence toward Nafinger's.

It hurt Sexton to see the waste and suffering. Refusing yet to blame himself entirely, he cursed Irv Stalcup.

The bawling of the new herd came when the Sextons were approaching the house. They stopped to listen. Irv must be bringing everything he had this time.

Sexton had already shifted his defense to the house, knowing that the loft of the barn would be a death trap when Irv's men worked in close to it.

Roman was scared. "Maybe old Belknap —"

"He's not coming." Belknap was a cowman. He had refused to be tolled into this fight. The angry side of Sexton's mind condemned the man. The thinking side admitted the logic of Belknap's stand.

At least Malcolm was safe at the K.

Moira was standing in the yard, a scarf around her dark hair. She too was listening to the herd.

"Get the wagon ready, Roman," Sexton said.

"Why?" Moira asked quickly.

"You're leaving right away."

The woman gave Sexton a calm look. She walked into the house. Something in her attitude made Roman hesitate. "Get the wagon ready, I said!" Sexton pointed toward the barn. His son went to obey.

Inside, Sexton lost for a time his decisiveness. He watched Moira wandering through the house with apparent aimlessness. She looked at the cooking utensils in the kitchen. She straightened a towel that had been jammed hastily on its rack. She stood for a moment in the doorway of the room where Mary had died. Waiting in the living room, Sexton saw her bend and make a tiny smoothing of the blankets on Roman's bed. She trailed her fingers along the smooth stones of the fireplace. She was smiling gently when she at last came to her husband.

"Get ready, Moira. Once it starts, I won't have time to get you away."

"Is there any chance to beat them?"

"Hell yes, there is. I can't turn back the herd, but I can stop enough men so they won't stay too long."

Moira received the lie with the same faint smile. She walked across the room and picked up a rifle. "What ever made you think I'd leave?" She looked from a window, sighting the rifle as calmly as a man.

"No, Moira! You've got to leave. There isn't a chance —"

"I know that, John. Show me which cartridges go into this, please."

She was not pretending and she was no longer opposing Sexton. He knew that instantly, and the knowledge shook him. She had fought against him to the last moment, and now, having lost, she would fight with him. They could not win. They both knew it, but she was accepting the fact more calmly than Sexton.

"Show me how to work this, John. I'll do what I can. Your hay is lost but maybe we can scare them away, you and Roman and I."

"No!" Sexton cried, and now he did not want Roman here either. The madness of his whole plan came down on him at once. He saw the folly and the revenge-driven greed of it; but still he had lived with the idea, feeding on it, and he could not discard it in a moment.

The fact remained that this was his land. The herd, sounding closer by the minute, and the men driving it were invaders coming to destroy him.

"I said get out of here, Moira."

The woman put the rifle down gingerly. She walked to Sexton slowly. "You know I can't."

"Why not?"

"After all these years you ask that?"

Her soft words pierced Sexton's bitterness and anger. The reply which he was ashamed to give while he was still twisted by indecision was like her question: the summing up of a lifetime.

Since last summer he had lived falsely, snarling at those who opposed him, combating himself. But even now if Moira had tried to force the admission from him, he would have stiffened against her. She merely looked at him, pouring out an understanding and trust beyond reason.

Roman called, "Dad! Dad! There's two of them out east and two more coming up from Nafinger's!"

Sexton gave himself no time to think. He grabbed his rifle and ran outside, and Moira followed him. Two men were standing by their horses on the east ridge, waiting, out of range. Two riders were coming full tilt from the south, bearing straight toward the house.

The leaders of the herd broke into sight on a ridge to the west. *Maybe it's too late,* Sexton thought.

An instant later Roman cried, "That's Cabot and Helen down there!"

The herd was twisting off the ridge when Cabot and Helen Belknap whirled into the yard.

"Did your father get my word?" Sexton shouted.

"Yes." Helen kept looking at Moira. "He wasn't doing anything about it when my mother and I left."

Cabot walked close to his father. "Mac is at the Renault place. He's been shot. Mrs. Belknap and Dr. McRae and Howell are with him." Cabot threw his accusing stare hard into the look of shock on Sexton's features.

Moira's face was gray. "How is he, Cabot?"

Still looking at his father, Cabot spoke carefully. "McRae said it was mostly shock and exposure. He walked several miles after he was shot." He looked at the herd, at the men on the hills. He drew a deep breath and was framing something bitter and explosive when Moira stepped between him and Sexton.

She put her hand on Cabot's arm and said something to him that Sexton had no will to hear as he stared at the rifle in his hands.

"Who did it, Cabot?" Roman asked.

"Champe. Mac couldn't talk until today. Champe did it. He killed Thurman afterward and Morse Hazel, and then he burned the house. Mac pretended like he was dead. Champ left him in the yard. Malcolm crawled into the barn, and that's where we found him when I came back from town. For a while we thought . . . That's where he is now." Cabot's voice rose. "In a filthy, cold barn, and all because —"

Once more Moira quieted him with soft words that Sexton did not hear.

Cabot's story made a confused picture in

Sexton's mind, but some aspects were horribly clear. Malcolm stumbling through the snow, crawling into a barn like a dying dog. The blame was on Jim Champe. He had never even come here to ask about hay because he must have known what the answer would be.

— *The blame is on me,* Sexton thought. *I have done my best to destroy my whole family.* He looked at Moira, prepared for the condemnation in her eyes. There was none.

Slowly, as if the herd no longer mattered, Sexton glanced across the fields to where men were tearing down his south fence. He said, "Moira, go to Malcolm as fast as you can."

"The doctor is there. I'll stay here."

Still angry, but with a sort of resignation behind his expression, Cabot walked to his horse and pulled a carbine from a scabbard. He said, "Beat it, Helen."

The girl was watching Moira. "I don't think I will, Cabot."

Sexton looked at everyone around him, a slow survey of faces and expressions that had seemed strange before. For the first time in months he saw people that he loved, instead of angry instruments trying to thwart him. He was like a man who had recovered suddenly from a great sickness.

Deliberately he held the sniper's rifle out to Moira. She took it. He saw tears in her eyes, but there was also a proud and steady look that made him humble.

"I'll go to Malcolm now," she said.

Sexton turned to Cabot. "Lend me your horse, son."

Sexton rode toward the broken fence where riders were crowding cows onto his land. The first man he passed was Stan Elwood. There was nothing to say. Sexton rode on. Irv Stalcup's sheepskin gave him enormous bulk as he waited, cold-faced with suspicion.

"Instead of breaking the fences around those stackyards," Sexton said, "pull the staples and untwist the wire. If you're short of tools you'll find plenty at the house."

Behind Sexton, Will Stalcup laughed. "Look who's making the offer now! I've waited —"

"Shut up, Will," Irv said. He studied Sexton narrowly and found no trickery in him; and he saw no defeat either. And that last pleased Irv Stalcup, who had no respect for failure. "All right, Sexton, we'll do that."

"The hay will be three dollars a ton, the same as I offered it to Belknap."

Irv wanted to flare up. He started to. He had good reasons and now he balanced them, challenging Sexton. Elwood was one of the reasons. Irv looked at him, and for a moment a precarious balance held.

Elwood jerked his head suddenly, looking toward the west hills. He pointed. Belknap and ten or twelve of his crew had come to the top of the ridge and were looking down on the situation.

Sexton stood high in the stirrups and signaled them away with a pushing motion of his arm.

"Oh!" Irv said. "You knew he was coming."

Sexton shook his head. "I thought he wasn't."

Once more Irv recognized the truth. "Well, by God," he said, and that covered everything he felt.

"You understand the price?"

Irv nodded. "We'll get along, but that's all, Sexton. Don't ever try to get friendly with me."

Sexton set a zigzag course between his stackyards on his way to overtake the wagon already moving down the valley. He looked back. Belknap and Cummerford were crowding through the fence with the rush of cows. The rest of the K riders were turning toward home.

Sexton took one brief look at the mattress and pile of blankets in the wagon box. Moira was driving, with Helen beside her.

Cabot and Roman were racing through the snow far ahead, Cabot on his father's horse.

Moira said, "I think they're going after Champe. I'm afraid —"

"I'll take care of them." Sexton looked back. Belknap and Cummerford were coming hard, but he could not wait for them. He put the buckskin out with a jump.

Cabot and Roman rode like fiends. Sexton sent a long call down the wind to them, but they merely glanced back and kept going and he could not overtake them.

Nafinger's buildings were brown huddles against the snow. As Sexton went past he saw Nafinger trot out and look up and down the valley, at the riders ahead of Sexton, at the two men behind him. And then Nafinger, as if perplexed and anxious to have no part in something he did not understand, strode back into the house.

Sexton made a great gain on his sons when they had to get down to fight a stub-

290

born gate on the north line fence of the Renault place. He yelled again, but they mounted and rode on. But now he was so close they had no chance to get away to try any wild ideas they were carrying.

They contented themselves then with beating him to the burned house. Mort Howell had built a fire in the yard. He was arguing with Cabot and Roman when Sexton swung down. Howell said angrily, "I told you it's a matter of law, not you!"

"Then start to do something!" Cabot said.

Sexton was going toward the barn when Dr. McRae came out, buttoning his bearskin coat, staring a long moment at nothing while his fingers moved mechanically and the wind riffled his beard. His whole attitude struck terror in Sexton, who was afraid to speak.

At last McRae gave him a sharp look and motioned him toward the fire. The five men stood in a circle, Cabot and Roman glowering at Howell. McRae spread his hands toward the warmth, studying Sexton bleakly.

"He'll be all right, I think," the doctor said. "He should be half dead of pneumonia, but his chest is clear. That boy has had a hellish time, Sexton." McRae put the blame where it belonged.

"Can I see him?"

"Yes." McRae looked at Sexton's sons. "The pair of you might get some of the blood lust out of your systems and go in too. He's been worrying about you."

Belknap and Cummerford rode up as the Sextons were going toward the barn. Belknap said, "Is my wife still here?"

"In the barn," McRae answered.

"What did you do with Nichols?" Cummerford asked.

Howell said, "He's over east. He'll be back."

Heavily wrapped in blankets, Malcolm lay on a pile of hay with Mrs. Belknap sitting beside him. The Sextons removed their hats. John Sexton greeted the woman as he knelt beside his son. Malcolm had been dozing. His eyes opened and he recognized his father, but small panic ran across his expression before he saw that his brothers were present also.

Since last summer he's grown away from me, Sexton thought, *and he had good reason, too. He may never fully trust me or love me again.* This was the first hard payment Sexton knew that he would make for his madness.

Before the Sextons left, the father said to

Mrs. Belknap, "Why don't you go out to the fire and get warm?"

She shook her head. "I'm snug enough. If I stir about I'll be cold. How soon will Moira and Helen —"

"Pretty quick," Sexton said.

Mrs. Belknap looked at Cabot. "Speak to my husband about the plans you and Helen had." Her color did not change. She gave no indication of confusion because she had shifted ground.

"Yes, ma'am," Cabot mumbled. She was on his side; he could not understand how it had come about.

The Sextons were quiet when they walked outside. They stood for a moment looking at each other, solidly bound together now. Quite simply Sexton said, "You can start building a new house here whenever you're set, Cabot."

Belknap heard the remark. In the act of lighting a cigar, he looked across his shoulder. When the Sextons came to the fire, he said, "Ride over and have a talk with me, Cabot, when you have the time."

There was a short silence. Everyone knew that a great deal had been settled.

Mort Howell spoke of what was yet unsettled. "Champe was moving cows this way three days ago. He's got guts to keep right on coming, especially if he don't know that the boy in there talked to us. I sent Nichols out to scout around. We'll wait until we hear from him." He spoke with determination, but he fell short of getting into his tone the authority he tried to express.

And so he added, "We've got to follow the law."

His last words sank away into a deep silence. Everyone had listened to them, but everyone looked to John Sexton for the decision.

It was a long time before he gave it. "All right, Howell, we'll follow the law." Sexton put his hand on Cabot's shoulder when he saw the flash of anger in his son's eyes.

Howell gave Sexton a grateful look; but at once, with full authority now on him, the deputy looked more gloomy than before.

Tracy Cummerford, the only pistolman in the group, ran his little test. He said casually, "Would you go after him alone, Howell?"

"Afraid as I am, I would, if I had to."

Cummerford nodded; he was satisfied.

The wagon came and the women went inside. It was then that Mrs. Belknap came out to warm herself. The men made room for her instantly. Belknap trotted off to drag charred wood from the house to build up the fire. Afterward he stood with the cigar in his teeth, brushing blackness from his gloves, watching his wife with a bemused, half smiling expression.

They bedded Malcolm warmly in hay piled upon the mattress in the wagon. Moira said to Belknap, "Rose and Helen are going to stay with me a few days."

Belknap made a half bow. "That's fine, Moira."

Ready to go, Moira looked at her husband thoughtfully. "I suppose you and the boys will be home when you get there."

Sexton nodded. The wagon crunched away. With a strange sense of wonder Sexton looked around him, at the burned house, at the rat-chewed tarpaulin that covered two dead men, at the living men with work yet to do.

Under these circumstances, with a few words and her expression, Moira had made the final tiny adjustment that set him again in the channel of a normal life. His own scars would be long with him, but the swift tomorrows would hide Moira's very soon.

Sexton watched the wagon for a long time and then went back to the fire. Cabot was saying, "I still think he burned the town."

"You don't know it, though," Howell said. "You're only reasonably sure you saw him crossing the street."

"Burned the town? I never heard about that," Sexton said. "You mean Champe?"

Howell gave Sexton an odd look. "Yeah. He had a grudge against Lew Glinkman. He could have done it, but we don't know that he did."

Sexton's feeling of guilt was already such that he was willing to make a fact from little evidence: Champe probably had burned the town. Now Sexton would have to do something to make up Glinkman's loss. That was as far as he would go. He could not be responsible for the world.

Cummerford turned his back to the fire. "If I'd known we were going to camp here, I'd have brought some coffee. How far did you tell Rusty to go, Howell?"

"I told him to use his judgment."

"Then he's headed for a saloon."

They huddled around the fire, stepping back from the smoke whips that hit them across the eyes, watching the snowfields to the east.

Belknap said: "I assume, John, that the Stalcups will winter on your place until the range is open. You and I had an agreement but I'm willing to switch. This place is too small, however —"

"There's the whole valley," Sexton said. "Nafinger and Lindstrom probably will be glad to winter cows. I'll tear up the options and let them sell their hay any way they see fit."

"That's fine." Belknap nodded.

Bundled to the ears, carrying a muzzle-loading rifle awkwardly across the saddle, Bill Nafinger rode up on a shaggy, unshod horse. He dismounted clumsily and came to the fire. "The wagon stopped. I thought some help might be needed here."

Howell eyed the serious, snow-burned face with its apologetic expression. He stared at the relic of a rifle. He did not know quite what to say.

Sexton said: "Bill, I'm dropping that crazy hay option. Can you winter cattle on your land until spring?"

"I sure can. Whose cows?"

"Some of mine," Belknap said. He stepped crisply into the details and the matter was settled in a few minutes.

"Have you got time to ride down and tell Lindstrom about it?" Sexton asked Nafinger. "There might be some cows for him too."

The others put no weight upon Na-finger. They did not look at him, and yet the insistence was there: he did not belong with this group in the matter they were waiting to start. Nafinger was sensible enough to make no false comments. He said, "I'll go see Donn," and rode away.

Sexton said: "He came. That's something to bear in mind."

A half-hour later they saw Rusty Nichols coming from the east. He dismounted and warmed his hands and rolled a cigarette, making them wait. Cabot and Roman stirred impatiently.

Squatted by the fire, Rusty said: "They're bringing the herd. Champe and six men." He blew smoke from his nostrils and stared over to where Thurman and Hazel lay under the tattered canvas.

"Since he's coming right to us —" Sexton said, and then he remembered that he had left everything to Howell. "What about it, Mort?"

Howell swallowed. "He's got guts." He was worried. "Do you suppose there's something wrong? Maybe Hazel and Thur-man got into it and —"

"You heard what my brother said." There was no doubt in Cabot's attitude. "You heard him."

"Yeah." Howell sighed. "All right, let's wait and let him come. I'm going to talk to him before anybody gets excited. Everybody understand that."

"Sure." Cummerford turned his back and looked across the fields with a half-smile.

Rusty looked at Sexton. "I left the gate by the creek open. All right?"

Sexton nodded. It was going to be a wasteful business. No stackyard fences. Stacks would be undercut and tumbled down and trampled from hell to breakfast. But the cows would survive.

The herd came in sight, tumbling off a windswept ridge, plowing a crooked furrow toward the valley.

"I'll go down and meet him and tell him it's all right to bring the cows in," Howell said.

When Howell led his horse from the barn, Sexton observed that the deputy had a sawed-down shotgun tied at the saddle horn. Howell hesitated once, glancing at the group around the fire. No one spoke. He swung up and rode to meet Champe.

The herd came through, rocking the gateposts as the cows crowded their way, and then, bellowing, the starving animals lunged through the snow toward the stacks. One of Champe's men pulled down panels of fence on both sides of the gate to relieve the bottleneck.

Presently Champe and Howell rode up to the group at the fire. Sexton kept studying the Five Bar owner. The man's outer bearing was sure, but there was still a tightness in his manner, as if he knew how thin the gamble was.

It was no longer last summer that counted against Jim Champe in Sexton's mind. That part was laid forever in the past. Champe's guilt was right here.

But the way the man made his play raised a doubt in Sexton's thinking.

"Mort's been telling me," Champe said. He looked at the burned house. "That God-damned Hazel. I told him to size the place up, and that was all." He swung down and went to the tarpaulin.

He moved the scrap iron that held the edge down. He lifted one side of the canvas and had his look, and when he dropped the tarp and put the weight back his face was hideous with shock and revulsion.

Champe stepped back. He looked at the quiet men who had moved away from the fire. "So help me God, boys, I told Morse not to try anything, just to look around and see what chance we had to get in here without a fight. I won't say that I wouldn't have made a fight of it, if that was the way it stacked up . . ." He shook his head, standing with his hands in his coat pockets.

Sexton had not heard Malcolm's words. Hurt and dazed Malcolm could have told a garbled story. Sexton saw the shadow of doubt on Cabot's face, and Cabot had heard the story firsthand. Belknap gave Sexton an inquiring look. Belknap was not sure either.

And it was apparent that Howell was confused too. He stood apart from the others, holding his shotgun. It was his play. At last he said, "You're under arrest, Champe, until we get this straightened out."

"Under arrest! My God! What for? Morse Hazel run hog-wild, but I didn't tell him to do it." He was outraged. He made his words most plausible. "Nobody is even sure what happened here. You said so yourself."

The Indian cast of Tracy Cummerford's face was like dark stone. His eyes held Champe in a narrow grip. "The kid ain't dead, Champe. He told everything."

"What kid?" Champe said it too fast, and it came with a rising edge of voice, and all the tightness of his brain was in his trapped and savage manner as he looked at the cold faces of the men scattered in the yard.

"What kid?" Champe destroyed the last threads of his own bluff, and the lie was no longer strong enough to cause hesitation in anyone's mind. One moment ago there had been doubt and a grudging adherence to law, but now the swollen weight of savagery was pulsing here.

Champe had been tried and convicted. He knew it. All his intentness fixed on John Sexton, the man he chose to take the dark trip with him.

Howell's lack of experience allowed the sharp instant for turning back violence to slip away.

Champe's pistol belt was under his buttoned sheepskin, but his pistol was in the hand that came from his coat pocket. He was nearly even with Cummerford. He was the merest brush of time behind Mort Howell, who was nervous and unsure.

Howell fired both barrels of his shotgun as he was bringing it up. The blast covered Cummerford's pistol shot as three barrels hurled their lead into Champe. The man went down and stained the snow, and the pistol he had tried to bear on Sexton was crushed out of sight beneath him.

Sexton had his own moment of dropping deep into blackness as he thought, *This could have been multiplied by ten if I had not been stopped.* He let his pistol fall back into the holster.

After a time Howell said: "I'll go talk to his men. When they know the truth, they won't have any reason for trying to make trouble."

"I'm sure of it," Belknap said. "But Tracy and I will go along with you anyway." He turned to Sexton. "Remember this, John, no matter where the urges came from, the man died of his own acts."

Sexton and Roman rode home without Cabot; he was a deputy with unpleasant chores to finish. But in a day or two he would be home, for a time at least.

The wind was steadily out of the northwest, and spring was a lonely thought buried deep in all the whiteness. At the Nafinger place the Sextons stopped when Mrs. Nafinger waved them in for coffee. They gave her the news and had little more to say, but she saw the change in Sexton, and when he rode away she smiled.

The sight of cattle in his own fields warmed the last of the bleakness from Sexton. The products of the earth grew to be used, a cycle that only a fool would try to disrupt. He looked through blowing snow at the grave on the distant hill and a touch of bitterness was still in him, but now it was from an honest loss and not from dishonest anger against mankind.

They rode on toward the house. The smoke lying on the wind out from the chimney was a banner of welcome. Sexton looked around his land. Spring, after all, was not far off; it never could be far away. He said, "We've got a lot of work to do before long, Roman."

With Moira beside him he knew he would never again try to turn his back on the land.